# BAD DAD

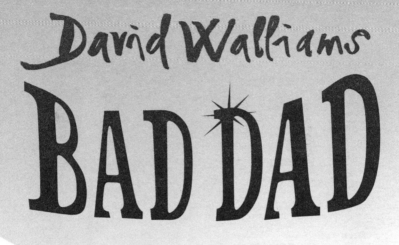

# David Walliams

# BAD DAD

*Illustrated by Tony Ross*

HarperCollins *Children's Books*

**HarperCollins** PUBLISHERS
Since 1817

First published in
Great Britain by HarperCollins *Children's Books* in 2017

HarperCollins *Children's Books* is a division of HarperCollins*Publishers* Ltd,
HarperCollins Publishers, 1 London Bridge Street, London SE1 9GF

The HarperCollins website address is:
www.harpercollins.co.uk

7

Text copyright © David Walliams 2017
Illustrations copyright © Tony Ross 2017
Cover lettering of author's name copyright © Quentin Blake 2017
All rights reserved.

HB ISBN 978–0–00–816465–2
TPB ISBN 978–0–00–825433–9

David Walliams and Tony Ross assert the moral right to be identified as
the author and illustrator of the work respectively.

Printed and bound in England by CPI Group (UK) Ltd,
Croydon CR0 4YY

MIX
Paper from
responsible sources
**FSC**
www.fsc.org   **FSC™ C007454**

This book is produced from independently certified FSC™ paper
to ensure responsible forest management.

For more information visit: www.harpercollins.co.uk/green

# THANK-YOUS

## I WOULD LIKE TO THANK:

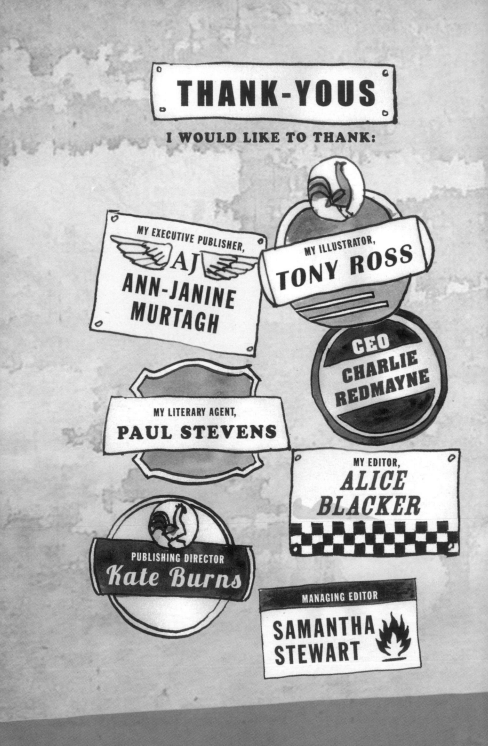

MY EXECUTIVE PUBLISHER,
**AJ**
**ANN-JANINE MURTAGH**

MY ILLUSTRATOR,
**TONY ROSS**

CEO
**CHARLIE REDMAYNE**

MY LITERARY AGENT,
**PAUL STEVENS**

MY EDITOR,
**ALICE BLACKER**

PUBLISHING DIRECTOR
*Kate Burns*

MANAGING EDITOR
**SAMANTHA STEWART**

CREATIVE DIRECTOR
**VAL BRATHWAITE**

TEXT DESIGNER
**ELORINE GRANT**

COVER DESIGNER
**KATE CLARKE**

MARKETING AND PR DIRECTOR
**GERALDINE STROUD**

AUDIO EDITOR
**TANYA HOUGHAM**

PUBLISHER
**RACHEL DENWOOD**

David Walliams

Dads come in all sorts of shapes and sizes. There are **FAT** ones and thin ones, tall ones and short ones. There are *young* ones and **old** ones, clever ones and stupid ones.

There are *silly* ones and **serious** ones, **LOUD** ones and quiet ones.

Of course there are good dads, and **bad dads**.

# This is the story of a dad and his son.

**Frank**
is the son.

Dad is the dad.
His name is
**Gilbert**.

This is **Rita,**
Frank's mum.

**Auntie Flip** is Dad's aunt.
She babysits Frank sometimes.

**Mr Big** is a surprisingly small crime boss. Whatever time of day it is, he wears silk pyjamas and a dressing gown, with velvet slippers monogrammed "Mr B".

Mr Big has two henchmen, Fingers and Thumbs.

**Fingers** is so called for his long, thin fingers, perfect for picking pockets.

**Thumbs** has enormous thumbs that he uses to inflict terrible pain on Mr Big's enemies.

**Will** and **Bear**
are Thumbs's fearsome nephews.

**Chang** is
Mr Big's
sinister butler.

**Reverend Judith** is a vicar.

**Sergeant Scoff** is the
local policeman.

**Mr Swivel** is a one-eyed
prison guard.

**Judge Pillar** is well known for having a heart of stone.

**Raj** is a newsagent.

# This is a map of the town.

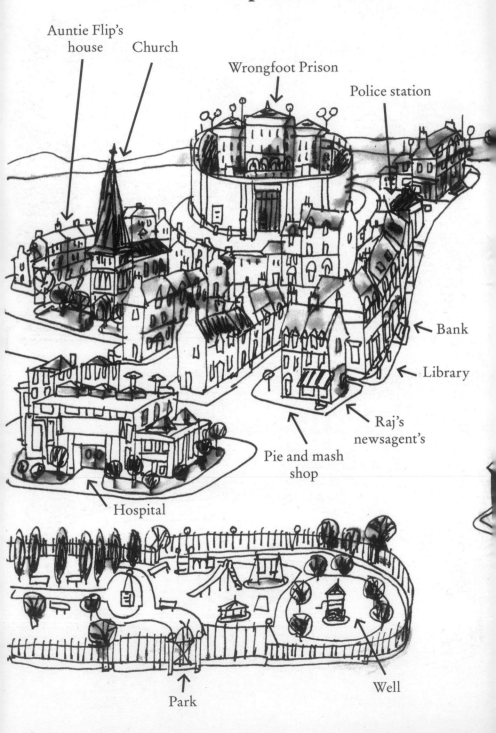

Auntie Flip's house

Church

Wrongfoot Prison

Police station

Bank

Library

Raj's newsagent's

Pie and mash shop

Hospital

Park

Well

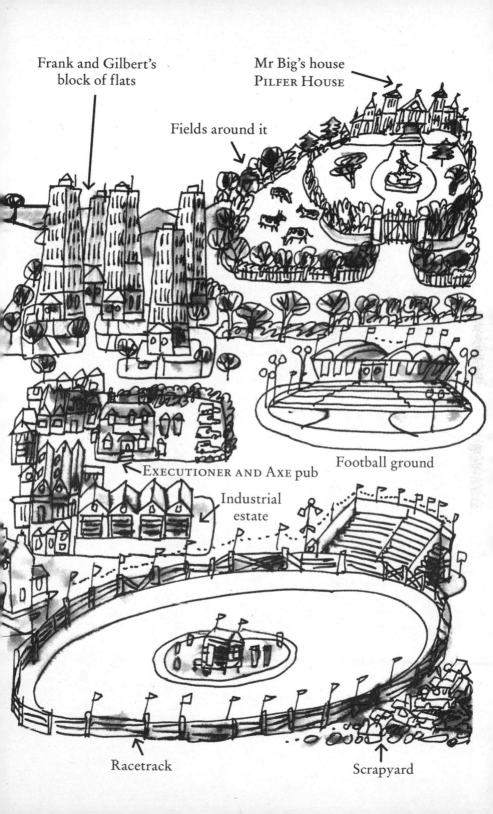

Frank and Gilbert's
block of flats

Mr Big's house
PILFER HOUSE

Fields around it

EXECUTIONER AND AXE pub

Football ground

Industrial
estate

Racetrack

Scrapyard

# CHAPTER

# 1

# ROAR!

*ROAR!* went Dad's car as it sped round the dirt track. Frank's father was a banger racer. It was a dangerous sport. Cars would *smash* into each other...

*BANG!*

**WALLOP!**

*CRUNCH!*

...as they **zoomed** round and round.

Dad raced an old Mini that he had souped up himself. He had painted a Union Jack on the car, and named her **"Queenie"** after a lady he admired, Her Majesty the Queen. The car became as famous in racing circles as Dad. **Queenie's** engine made an unmistakable sound like a lion. *ROAR!*

Dad was **King of the Track**. He was the greatest banger racer the town had ever seen. People came from all over the country to watch him race. Nobody won more times than him. Week after week, month after month, year after year, Dad would lift the trophies above his head as the crowds cheered and shouted his name.

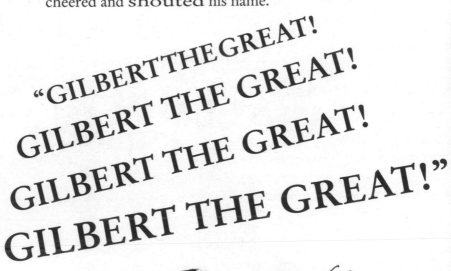

"GILBERT THE GREAT! GILBERT THE GREAT! GILBERT THE GREAT! GILBERT THE GREAT!"

*Life was golden.* Because Dad was a local hero, everyone wanted to know him. Whenever he took his son out for pie and mash, the owner of the shop would give them double helpings and then wouldn't let them pay a penny. If Frank was walking down the street with his father, people in cars would beep their horns…

## BEEP! BEEP!

…and smile and wave. The boy always felt a burst of pride whenever that happened. Frank even got marked up on a test by his Maths teacher after the

man got a photo taken with his father at parents' evening.

No one was a bigger fan of Dad than his own son.

The boy worshipped his father. He was a hero to him. Frank longed to be just like his dad one day, a champion race-car driver. His dream was to one day drive **Queenie**.

As you might expect, father and son looked alike. Both were short and round, with sticky-out ears. The boy looked like someone had put his dad into a shrinking machine. Of all the children at his school, Frank knew he was never going to be the tallest or the handsomest or the **strongest** or the cleverest or the funniest. But he had seen the magic and wonder his father could create with his skill and courage on the racetrack. More than anything, he wanted to taste that.

As for Dad, he forbade his son from watching him race. A night would start with twenty cars speeding round the track, and by the end there would be just one car still standing. Drivers often got badly injured in the pile-ups, and sometimes spectators did too if the cars crashed into the stands.

"It's dangerous, mate," said Dad. Gilbert always called his son "mate". They were father and son, but best friends too.

"But, Dad…" the boy would plead as his father tucked him up in bed.

"No 'buts', mate. I don't want you to see me get hurt."

"But you're the best! You'll never get hurt!"

"I said 'no buts'. Now come on, be a good boy.

Give us a **huggle**\* and go to sleep."

Dad would always plant a kiss on his son's forehead before he went out to race for the night. As for Frank, he would close his eyes and pretend to be asleep. However, as soon as he heard the door close, he would creep out of bed and crawl down the hallway to the front door so as not to alert his mum. The woman would always shut herself in her bedroom and speak in hushed tones on the telephone whenever her husband was out of the house. Still dressed in his pyjamas, the boy would run all the way to the racetrack.

Just outside the stadium was a huge tower of rusty old cars that had been smashed up in previous races. Frank would climb to the top of the pile. There he had the best view of the race. The boy would sit cross-legged on the roof of the highest car, and watch all the bangers speed by. Every time his father's Mini, **Queenie**, zoomed past, *roaring* as she went, the boy would cheer.

---

\* A huggle was what the pair called their special embrace. It was halfway between a hug and a cuddle, hence the name.

Dad had no idea his son was up there. The man barred his son from watching him race because he feared the worst might happen. **One night it did.**

# CHAPTER

# OUT OF CONTROL

The night of the accident there seemed to be something badly wrong with Dad's car from the start. Instead of the Mini's distinctive roar, today the engine was making a loud grinding noise, as if it was about to explode.

As soon as Dad threw **Queenie** into gear on the start line, the car lurched forward in stops and starts like a bucking bull.

That fateful night, Frank was sitting on top of the pile of cars just outside the stadium as he always did. It was in the depths of winter, and wind and rain swirled around him. Despite being soaked to the skin, the boy never wanted to miss a race.

Something was wrong that night. Very wrong.

As soon as the flag waved to start the race, Dad struggled to control his own car.

Tonight there was no roar from the Mini's engine, rather that grinding noise. A deathly hush descended on the crowd. Frank felt sick to his stomach.

Suddenly there was a huge explosion from **Queenie's** exhaust pipe.

# *BANG!*

"DAD!" shouted the boy. From all that distance the man couldn't hear his son, especially over the thunder of all the other cars' engines. Frank desperately wanted to help. To do something. Anything. But he was powerless to stop what was about to happen.

The Mini sped up dramatically, and then wouldn't slow down. It was out of control.

# *ZOOM!*

The art of racing motor vehicles is knowing when to go fast, and when to slow down. Immediately, Dad was taking the corners far too quickly. This wasn't what a champion banger racer did. Frank's heart was thumping in his chest. **Queenie's** brakes must have gone. But how? Dad would always check and recheck his car before every race.

Suddenly, **Queenie** *swerved* sharply to avoid a head-on collision with a Ford Capri. But the Mini

was going far too fast, and as it turned it rolled

over and over and over.

BOOM! BOOM! BOOM!

Dad's car was now upside down in the middle of the track. The Jaguar behind smashed into the Mini, sending the car flying through the air. It crashed to the ground again…

# BAMM!

…smashing into pieces.

"NO, DAD, NO!" shouted Frank from the top of the tower of cars.

Down on the track there was a mighty pile-up as the cars couldn't stop in time.

## SMASH!
## BANG!
## CRASH!

There was the sound of metal crunching into metal and glass smashing.

# *KABOOM!*
### One of the cars exploded into a fireball!

"NOOOO!" shouted Frank.

The boy raced down the tower of cars, and ran through the crowds to his dad's car. An air ambulance hovered overhead before landing on the track. Frank held his father's hand through the wreckage, as the firemen tried to cut him out of the car.

"What are you doing here, mate?" whispered Dad. "You should be at home in bed."

"I'm sorry, Dad," replied Frank.

"I'm going to need the biggest **huggle** when I am out of this."

"Everything's going to be all right, Dad. I *promise*."

But it was a *promise* the boy couldn't keep.

# CHAPTER 3

# CRUSHED IN THE CRASH

## *NEE-NAW! NEE-NAW!*

Frank held his father's hand as the ambulance raced to the hospital. The man's right leg had been completely crushed in the crash, and he was losing a lot of blood.

"Mr Goodie," began the doctor as soon as Dad had been rushed into the Accident and Emergency department at the hospital. "I have some very bad news. We have to amputate your leg."

"Which one?" replied Dad, not losing his sense of humour at this dark time.

"The right one, of course. If we don't operate straight away, there is a very real chance you will die."

"I don't want you to die, Dad!" said Frank.

"It's all right, mate. I'm good at hopping."

As Dad was immediately taken down to the operating theatre, Frank tried and tried to call his mother, but the line was engaged for hours. The operation took all night. Frank paced up and down the waiting area, unable to sleep. When his father came to from the anaesthetic in the morning, his son was the first person he saw when he opened his eyes.

"Mate, you're the best," whispered Dad. It was clear he was in a lot of pain.

"I am so pleased you made it, Dad," replied Frank.

"Of course. I didn't want to miss seeing you grow up. Where's your mother?"

"I don't know, Dad. I called and called her last night, but I couldn't get through."

"She'll come."

It was a couple of hours until she did.

"Oh, Gilbert!" she said upon seeing him, and burst into tears.

The family reunion was brief, though, as she didn't stay that long.

Gilbert was in hospital for months, but his wife's visits to his bedside became less and less frequent, and shorter and shorter. However, the nurses set up a little camp bed for Frank, and the boy slept by his father's side every single night.

One day the doctors came in with a wooden leg for Gilbert. It fitted him perfectly. Within days he learned to walk again, and insisted on walking all the way back to their block of flats from the hospital.

"I can still do everything!" said Dad proudly.

He walked with a limp, and Frank held his hand the whole way, but they got home eventually.

When they arrived back at the flat, Mum wasn't there. She had left a note on the kitchen table. It read:

To Frank and Gilbert, I am sorry. Rita

# CHAPTER

4

# HARD-FACED MEN

"What does it mean, Dad?" asked Frank. "Why is she sorry?"

"Because she has left."

"She's not coming back?"

"No."

"Why?"

"Your mum has gone to live in a **big house** with a small man."

"But…!"

"I'm sorry, Frank. I tried my best for her. But my best wasn't good enough."

"I'm sorry, Dad."

"I need a **huggle**."

"Me too."

Father and son held on to each other tight, and they cried and cried until they could cry no more.

To his credit, Dad never said anything bad about his wife – or by this time ex-wife – but Frank felt deeply hurt that his mother had left without even saying goodbye.

Even though she now lived in a huge house, Mum never invited her son to stay. Not once. When she forgot her son's birthday for the second year in a row, Frank was in no hurry to see his mother again. Weeks and months passed without any contact, and then it became unthinkable to call her. So he never did.

Frank never stopped thinking about her, however. It was confusing because, as much as she'd hurt him, **Frank still loved her.**

Dad lost so much after the crash. Not just his leg, but his wife too. Soon he was about to lose something else dear to him.

**His job.**

Gilbert loved being a banger-racing driver. It was all he'd dreamed of from when he was a boy. Despite his pleas, the track owners banned him from racing ever again. They blamed him for the accident, and never wanted to see him back on the track. What's more, they told him it wasn't safe for him to race cars with only one leg.

So Dad tried and tried to get a different job, any job. But jobs in the town were scarce, and a man with a wooden leg always found himself at the bottom of the pile.

Dad was used to being a hero, but now he felt like a zero.

Two cold Christmases came and went. As time passed, Frank became increasingly worried about his father. Sometimes he would find the man sitting alone in an armchair, staring into space. Often Dad wouldn't leave the flat they lived in for days.

No one beeped their horns any more when they walked down the street, and now they couldn't afford to go to the **pie and mash shop**, let alone be given double helpings.

On Frank's eleventh birthday, Dad bought his son a huge race-car set. The boy loved it.

It was the best toy ever. Dad even painted one of the miniature Minis with a Union Jack so it looked just like **Queenie**. Together they would play with it late into the night, re-enacting Dad's famous victories on the track.

However, as much as he loved it, Frank worried where his father, who'd been unemployed now for a couple of years, had got the money from to buy it. Frank knew that very few children had toys like these. Race-car sets cost hundreds of pounds. And Dad didn't have hundreds of pounds.

Soon after Frank's birthday, groups of **hard-faced** men started banging on the door of the flat.

*THUD! THUD! THUD!*

They would wave pieces of paper and bark about "unpaid debts". Then they would push past Frank and force their way in. Once inside, the men would pick up anything they thought might be worth something, and march out with it. First it was the TV, then it was the sofa, then it was the boy's bunk bed.

One time Frank wouldn't answer the door and they simply smashed it off its hinges. That day they took the toy race-car track.

After these visits, Dad would become full of sorrow. A look of despair would cross his face, and he would sit in silence. Frank would do his best to cheer up his sad dad.

"Don't be down, Dad," the boy would say. "I will get all our stuff back one day. I promise. When I'm grown up, I will become a racing driver just like you."

"Come here, son, and give us a **huggle**."

The pair would embrace, and everything would feel all right again. They may have been poor, but

Frank never felt poor in his heart. The boy didn't mind that his jumpers had so many holes in them they were more hole than jumper. He never cared that he had to carry his books to school in a plastic bag that always broke. Soon it became normal that they had just one working light bulb in the flat and they had to move it from room to room at night.

That is because the boy had the best dad in the world. Or so he thought.

# CHAPTER

**5**

# TOP SECRET

One night over a dinner of cold baked beans in their cold flat, Dad made an announcement.

"Everything is about to change."

A concerned look crossed Frank's face. Despite having nothing, the boy liked things just the way they were. Dad rested his hand on his son's shoulder.

"It's nothing to worry about, mate. Everything is about to change for the better."

"But how?"

"Our life is about to change. I've got a job."

"Brilliant, Dad! I'm so happy for you!"

"I'm happy too," replied the man, though somehow he didn't look it.

"What's the job?"

"Driving."

"Banger racing?" asked Frank excitedly.

"No," said Dad. He gathered his thoughts. "But I will be driving fast. *Very fast.*"

"Wow!" The boy's eyes lit up like headlights on a motor car.

"Yeah! Wow! And I will be earning money. Lots of money. We can get the TV back."

"The TV is boring. I like listening to all your racing stories."

"All right, then, mate, we can get the sofa back!"

The boy thought for a moment. It wasn't comfortable eating dinner sitting on a wooden crate. "I don't mind the splinters in my bottom!"

"Really?" asked Dad with a chuckle. As the man laughed, he rocked back and forth on the crate.

"*Ouch!* I've got another one!"

"Ha! Ha!"

"All right, all right. I know what you really want back."

"What?"

"Your race-car set."

The boy fell silent. He did miss that toy very much. "I guess, Dad."

"I'm really sorry they took that away, mate."

"Don't worry, Dad."

Frank could tell something was up with his father – he just couldn't tell what. What was this mysterious job?

"So what will you be driving, Dad? Race cars?"

"No, this is driving just as fast but on real roads."

"Ambulances?"

"No."

"FIRE ENGINES?"

"No."

The boy's eyes widened. "Not for the police?"

Dad managed to nod and shake his head at the same time. "That sort of thing, yeah."

The boy's brain braked. "Dad, what do you mean 'that sort of thing'?"

"Well, it's TOP SECRET."

"TELL ME!" demanded the boy.

"It wouldn't be TOP SECRET if I told you!"

"Well, it would be very nearly TOP SECRET."

"I can't, mate. Sorry. But I am going to get paid. Big money. Really big money. And we are going to have stuff. Lots and lots of stuff. New trainers, toys, computer games, whatever you want."

Frank watched with concern as his dad's eyes widened. It all sounded too good to be true.

"But I don't need lots of stuff, Dad. All I need is you."

This burst Dad's balloon. "Yeah, yeah. Don't you

worry. I'll be here. I ain't going anywhere."

"You promise?"

"Yeah, yeah. I promise, mate."

"And you aren't going to get hurt?" asked the boy. The last thing he wanted was for his dad to lose his left leg.

"*Promise!*" said Dad. He held up three fingers on his right hand. "Scout's honour! Ha! Ha!"

"You were never a Scout!"

"It don't matter. Now finish up those baked beans. I need you to go to bed!"

Like all children in the world, Frank knew exactly what time his bedtime was and it wasn't now. "But it's not my bedtime yet!" he protested.

"By the time you are ready for bed, it will be."

That logic, although sound, was deeply annoying. "Not fair! Why do I have to go to bed now?"

"Auntie Flip will be here any minute to look after you."

"Oh no," replied Frank.

"Don't be like that. She's the only family we've got. And, best of all, she is always up for babysitting."

"I'm not a baby."

"I know that, mate."

"And why is it called 'babysitting'? You mustn't sit on a baby."

"Ha! Ha!" Dad laughed. "I dunno!"

"Where are you going anyway?"

"I just have to pop out for a meeting at the boozer."

"Can I come, Dad?"

"NO!"

"PLEASE?" pleaded the boy.

"No! This is grown-ups' stuff. Kids aren't allowed down the boozer anyhow."

"But I want to come."

"Sorry, mate, you can't. Now come on, give us a huggle."

Tonight the huggle was tighter than usual. Dad always held his son a little tighter when he was feeling worried about something. Frank wasn't stupid. The boy knew something was up. He just didn't know what. Yet.

# THE SMELL OF OLD BOOKS

Auntie Flip wasn't Frank's aunt. She was Dad's aunt. "Flip" was short for Philippa, and she prided herself on being from the posh side of the family, even though there wasn't one. The lady had the smell of old books about her. That was probably because she was a librarian. Auntie Flip wore glasses with glass thicker than in a shark's tank. Her idea of an evening's entertainment was to bring a stack of her own unpublished poetry books over, and read them out loud to the boy.

Auntie Flip had written many volumes of poetry:

Frank hated poetry. Flip would read him her poems about clouds and gooseberries and rainy days and birdsong and talcum powder. For Frank, listening to them was **torture**.

That night the boy was annoyed that he was left alone with the woman while his dad went out for his really exciting top-secret, couldn't-even-tell-his-own-son meeting. Doing what he was told, Frank put his pyjamas on, and then popped his head round the door of the living room.

"Goodnight, Auntie Flip!" he said quickly, before turning to go.

"Not yet it isn't!" chirped the lady.

"Sorry?"

"As a very special treat, young man, I'm going to let you stay up late."

"COOL!" exclaimed the boy.

"Yes! You can stay up late so I can read you some of my poetry."

This was definitely not cool.

"I know how much you like it," she said.

"I'm really tired," lied Frank, pretending to yawn, and he stretched his arms out for good measure.

"You won't be in a moment, young man, because I have a surprise for you! Do you like surprises?"

"It depends. What is it?"

"If I told you, it wouldn't be a surprise!" replied Auntie Flip.

The boy thought for a moment. "Is it a poetry-based surprise?"

"Yes! How did you know?"

"It was just a wild guess," sighed Frank.

The lady clicked open her handbag, and took out her leather-bound notebook. She held it in her hands as if it was a holy relic. Carefully she turned the first page.

"The first one this evening is a poem I wrote about you, Frank."

Somehow the thought of a poem about himself made Frank squirm. It was a similar feeling of unease as the time when Frank ate some sausages in the school canteen that hadn't been cooked properly and he had to run to the toilet as he could feel his bottom was about to explode.

Auntie Flip started making strange sounds with her mouth. It was like the noise of a braying horse.

# "NEIGH! NEIGH!"

Next she began making humming noises in an ear-achingly high-pitched tone. It was like someone running their fingers along the rim of a glass.

"WEEEEEEE, WAAAAA, WEEEEEEEEEEEEEE, WAAAAAAAAAAAAAAA..."

Frank put his fingers in his ears. "Is this the poem?" he shouted over the din.

Flip looked at the boy as if he was bonkers.

"No! I am just warming up the voice! Right. I am ready. This one is entitled simply 'Frank', and it is by me.

"My lovely little Frank,

I want to say thank

You for being you,

The super-duper son

Of my only nephew.

You are a boy,

Who spreads joy,

Like a butterfly who dances on the breeze,

Or a hummingbird singing in the trees,

Or a dolphin leaping through the sea,

Or a bee buzzing with another bee.

You bring happiness to my heart,

Like a freshly baked apple tart

With lashings of piping-hot custard,

Much nicer than adding some mustard.

I know it is strange to mention mustard,

But it is the only thing that rhymes with custard.

Please, O Frank, don't ever get old –

Stay forever young and bold!

So my poem draws to a close.

One last thing: don't pick your nose."

The lady's eyes were glistening with tears at the *sheer beauty* of her own poem.

"Well?" she asked, through sniffs. Her eyes searched Frank's face for approval.

"Well, what?" asked the boy.

"Well, what did you think of your special poem?"

"Mmm. I thought the poem was very…"

"Yes?"

Frank was old enough to know sometimes you have to tell a little lie to save other people's feelings.

"Poetic! It was a very poetic poem."

The lady was overjoyed. "Thank you so much! That is high praise. Any poet wants their poems to be poetic. So one down, ninety-nine to go."

"I need to go to bed!"

"Are you sure?"

"Absolutely. I need to go to bed right now!"

"How about I read to you *'A Love of Mauve'*?"

"I would love to hear it, but…"

"Or *'Some Lines on My Foot Cheese'*?"

"I really couldn't…"

"You are going to adore **'*Ode to a Puddle*'**!
*Plop, plop, plop, the rain goes plop…*"

"NO! I mean… no."

The lady looked hurt. "What do you mean 'no'?"

"I mean thank you, but no. I just feel so emotional after listening to that beautiful one you wrote about me."

Auntie Flip nodded her head. "Of course! Of course. I forget the raw power of my verse. I bid you goodnight." The lady opened her arms to give the boy a hug. Reluctantly the boy paced towards her. She always squeezed him too tight.

"*URGH!*" said Frank, as he could feel the air being squashed out of him.

"Sorry," said Auntie Flip. "I am not good with hugs."

The lady had never been married, nor to Frank's knowledge ever had a romance. He guessed she hadn't had many hugs in her life.

"Goodnight," said the boy. "I am off to sleep now."

That was another lie.

**A big lie.**

# 7

# DEATH BY POETRY

Escaping from the flat was something Frank had done many times before. Years ago Frank would sneak past his mum every Saturday night to watch his father race.

Back then it was easy. Frank would prop up his pillows on his bed under the duvet. That way if Mum bothered to get off the phone and poke her head round the door she would think her son was lying there fast asleep. Now there were **no pillows, duvet** or, indeed, bed. Since the

**hard-faced** men had come, the boy had slept on an old Lilo that always deflated during the night like a long, slow trump.

Frank had to come up with a new plan, and fast. If he was forced to listen to one more of Auntie Flip's poems, there was a very real danger that he would spontaneously **combust**.

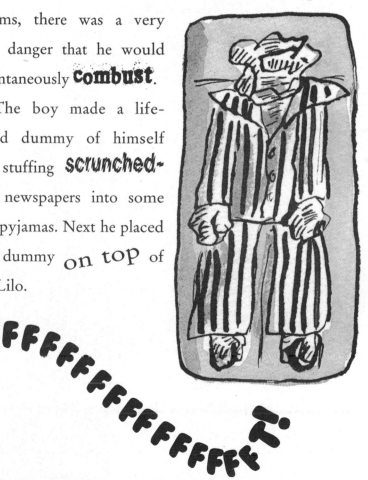

The boy made a life-sized dummy of himself by stuffing **scrunched-up** newspapers into some old pyjamas. Next he placed the dummy on top of his Lilo.

FFFFFFFFFFFFFFFFFFFFFFFFFFFFT!

Finally, Frank had to pick his moment to make his escape out through the front door. From his bedroom he could hear that – surprise, surprise – Auntie Flip was composing a new poem in the living room. She was reciting it out loud as she wrote.

*"O tall proud tree,*
*I see much of you in me,*
*Although I don't have leaves*
*Or branches for that matter,*
*And I am not made of wood,*
*But other than that I could*
*Be a tree. And, oh yes, I don't have bark…*

"Oh dear, no, let me start again.

*"O tall proud tree…"*

The living room was at the end of the hall, so there was every chance Auntie Flip would see Frank if he tried to make a dash for the front door. After a short while, the boy could hear the lady shuffle down the corridor. This was his chance! Frank opened his bedroom door a tiny bit and put his eyeball up to the crack. Auntie Flip was closing the toilet door behind her.

CL*IC*K!

"Oh no! The debt collectors have taken the loo seat too!" Frank heard her exclaim. "I will have to hover."

There was no way of Frank knowing if it was a number one or a number two. How could he know? Such a thing was a private matter between Auntie Flip and Auntie Flip's bottom.

A number two could take a long time (for some people hours, even days*) whereas a number one could be over in seconds. So Frank scuttled across the floorboards as quickly as he could (the **hard-faced** men had taken the carpet too) towards the front door. There he planned to wait for the noise of the flush to cover his escape.

---

* The longest recorded number two took four whole days to deliver. It was by fifty-stone opera tenor Antonio Lasagnotti. It was the length of a football pitch.

## DISASTER!

The toilet door opened again.

# CL*IC*K*!*

"I don't believe it! No loo roll!" muttered Auntie Flip to herself.

Frank was crouched in the hallway, but **scuttled** back to his bedroom just in time. With her bloomers still round her ankles Auntie Flip sc*a*mp*e*red side*ways* like a crab back to the living room.

"Now, which poem can I sacrifice?" she asked herself. "They are all masterpieces. Let me see. Oh yes, 'Ode to a Poached Egg' can go!"

The boy then heard a page being torn out of a book. R
I
P!

Flip then scuttled back to the toilet and closed the door. CLICK!

Frank crawled back to the front door and waited for the sound of the toilet flush.

CLUNK!

Flip pulled the chain. But nothing happened.

CLUNK!

Again. Nothing.

CLUNK! CLUNK! CLINK!

"Oh, goodness me! The chain's snapped!" she exclaimed.

The boy then heard effort noises coming from behind the toilet door. "I'll just have to hook my bloomers over the lever."

Success!

Frank opened the front door, and shut it behind him as quietly as he could.

CLUNK!

The lift was always broken in the block of flats, which was a pain when you lived on the ninety-ninth floor. Fortunately, Frank had devised a cool way of getting down the seemingly endless staircase. He'd found an old laundry basket, and with felt-tip pens had painted it with the colours of **Queenie** – red, white and blue. All he had to do was sit at the top of the staircase, and then let gravity take its course.

WHOOSH!

# CHAPTER 8

# FLYING VICAR

In no time at all, Frank was speeding down the staircase, and pretending he was a real-life racing driver. *THUNK!*
*THUNK!*
*THUNK!*

The washing basket juddered as it hit each step. Frank had to hold on tight or he might be thrown out.

WHOOSH!

Just as in a banger race, there were plenty of things to bash into. It was hard to steer a basket, but Frank did his best to lean left and *right*, narrowly missing:

a broken-down washing machine…

an upturned shopping trolley…

a *flock* of pigeons…

a TV that had been **kicked** in…

a delivery driver carrying a $\begin{smallmatrix}s\\t\\a\\c\\k\end{smallmatrix}$ of pizzas…

a crate of **empty** bottles…

and a tiny old lady who was being *dragged* up the stairs by three little dogs

One person was
not so lucky. That was
the local vicar, Reverend
Judith. Unfortunately for her,
Frank took a bend far *too*
*fast*, and bashed slap-bang into the lady.

# *BOOSH!*

"ARGH!" she cried as she shot up into the air.

## Look! A flying vicar!

The lady did a somersault (her first) and landed on
her bottom.

# SPLAT!

Fortunately for Frank, Reverend Judith was such a nice lady that she was the one who apologised.

"So sorry for being in your way!" called out the vicar.

"I am so sorry, Reverend Judith!" shouted back the boy as he continued speeding down the staircase.

"I hope to see you at church on Sunday!" added the lady hopefully, rubbing her bruised behind. The vicar was always at the tower block inviting the residents to her empty church, even though they never came. Frank felt sorry for the lady, though not sorry enough to get out of bed on a Sunday morning and go.

# WHOOSH!

The washing basket rattled down the last few steps and skidded across the concrete.

# WHIZZ!

Eventually it came to a stop. The boy hid the basket behind some bins, and then dashed off in the direction of the local pub, the **Executioner and Axe.**

As he peered in through the grimy window, Frank saw the pub was heaving. This was the grown-up world in all its glory. Men were arguing, women were fighting and everyone was drinking. The pub was so noisy it hardly seemed the most sensible place for a top-secret meeting. Try as he might, the boy couldn't spot his father anywhere.

Just as he was about to give up and head home, Frank heard **muffled** voices coming from the car park. The boy turned round to see some men sitting talking in a white Rolls-Royce. The Rolls-Royce stuck out, not just from its bay because of its size, but also because it was the kind of expensive car you never ever saw on an estate like this.

The boy couldn't make out the men too clearly as the car was full of cigar smoke. Frank edged his way round the other parked cars to get a little closer. He could just see the outline of his dad sitting in the driving seat. But who were the other men? And what was he doing in this hugely *expensive* car?

To try to hear what was being said, Frank climbed up on to the roof of the plumber's van parked next to the Rolls-Royce. But all he could hear was the occasional word. It sounded like the men were talking quietly so as not to be overheard.

The boy had come so far. He wasn't going to give up now. So, as delicately as he could, Frank stepped from the top of the van on to the roof of the Rolls-Royce. He lay down on top of the car so he could hear what was being said.

This would turn out to be a dangerous mistake.

# CHAPTER 9

# ONE JOB

"What if we get caught?" It was Frank's father speaking.

*Get caught doing what?* thought Frank as he lay on the roof of the Rolls-Royce, listening in.

"If you drive fast enough, no one will get caught," replied a man. "I have done all the research. I have plans of the inside. You will be in and out in two minutes."

"I ain't sure about this. It's much bigger than you told me. Just let me pay you back the money I borrowed from you. Please?" said Dad.

"I've heard that one a million times before from you."

"I will find a job."

"There are no jobs in this town, especially for someone who has to hop to get around."

There was a low rumble of mocking laughter from the two men in the back seats. **"Ha! Ha! Ha!"**

"You love your boy, don't you?" said the man.

Frank gulped. He was talking about him.

"Yeah, yeah, of course I do. I love him more than anything in the world. What's he got to do with all this?"

"I would hate for anything to happen to him."

**"You leave my boy out of this!"**

"Then do what I say."

**"If you ever do anything to hurt my boy, I'll…"**

"You'll what?" snarled the man in the front passenger seat. "Take off your false leg and kick me with it?"

The two men in the back laughed again.

# "Ha! Ha! Ha!"

"All right, all right," said Dad. "I'll do what you say. But just this once. One job, and then I am done."

"That wasn't too hard now, was it?" purred the man in the front seat. "So, Gilbert, I want you to show me that you can still drive, like in the old days."

"I can still drive all right. Leg or no leg."

"Then show me."

"Are you ready?"

"Yes."

"Hold on tight," replied Dad.

The huge Rolls-Royce engine *revved* up.

# BRUM BRUUMM BRUUMMM!

Then the back wheels spun furiously, and clouds of smoke filled the air. Frank couldn't help but **splutter** at the smell of burning rubber. The boy struggled to his feet so he could jump back on the van parked beside the car. But Dad was much too quick for him. **The Rolls-Royce raced off into the night with Frank standing on the roof!**

# CHAPTER 10

# NO TIME TO BREATHE

Frank **slammed** his body down on to the roof of the car and clung on for dear life. The Rolls-Royce had spun out of the pub car park, and in no time was speeding down the road at one hundred miles an hour. The boy's eyes were watering and his hair was sticking up on end. This was the most **dangerous** fairground ride of all time.

Of course Dad had no clue that his son was clinging on to the roof of the Rolls-Royce. If he had, the man would never have:

driven straight through a red light…

*WHIZZ!*

swerved sharply to overtake a bus…

SCREECH!

and crashed through a fence…

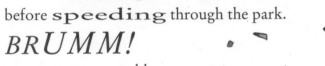

# *B A S H !*

before **speeding** through the park.

## *BRUMM!*

The Rolls-Royce bobbed up and down on the grass.

## *BOOM! BOOM! BOOM!*

The boy was bounced into the air, his body thumping up and down on the roof.

## *THUD! THUD! THUD!*

## "OOF! OOF! OOF!"

Just as he dared to open his eyes again, Frank saw that they were heading straight for another fence on the far side of the park.

# KABOOM!

Planks of wood **exploded** into the air. A large chunk **whizzed** past the top of Frank's head.

Everything was happening so fast that there was no time to breathe.

The car was heading straight towards an alleyway, which was much narrower than the car itself. If Dad didn't put on the brakes right now, it looked like the Rolls-Royce would **smash** slap-bang into a brick wall.

"STOP!" shouted the man in the passenger seat.

"ARGH!" screamed the pair in the back.

Instead the car's engine *revved* and sped up.

"NOOO!" came shouts from inside.

Frank couldn't take it any more. The boy had to close his eyes.

# TWO WHEELS ARE BETTER THAN FOUR!

On one side of the alleyway was a pile of planks of wood. The Rolls-Royce turned sharply and the wheels on the left side mounted the planks and it vaulted on to two wheels!

Frank opened his eyes again as he found himself sliding down the side of the roof. His fingers desperately clawed to get a grip.

Still on two wheels, the car just made it through the narrow alleyway. **WHIZZ!**

**"YOU'RE SQUASHING ME!"** came a shout from inside the car.

Bursting out of the other side of the alley, Dad turned the steering wheel sharply and the car bounced back down to four wheels. **BOINK!**

Just as Frank breathed a sigh
of relief, a siren blared.

## NEE-*NAW!*
## NEE-*NAW!*

Blue shadows flashed on the buildings around
them. The boy looked over his shoulder. A police car
was **chasing** after them.

Dad put his foot down on the accelerator, and
the Rolls-Royce whizzed off the wrong way down a
main road. Frank couldn't believe his eyes. The car
was weaving in and out of the traffic coming straight
at them! Lorries and cars swerved as Dad managed to

*twist* and **turn**
just in time.

It was ***thrilling*** and **terrifying** all at once.

Up ahead, a wall of flashing blue light was travelling

rapidly towards them. For a moment, Frank struggled

to work out what it was. He squinted. It was the POLICE! A line of police cars was travelling towards them at speed. They were driving in formation, blocking out the whole road.

**There was no way round them.**

**There was no way under them.**

**There was no way through them.**

**They were trapped.**

Dad was a champion race driver, but surely even he could not win this time.

Frank breathed a sigh of relief. This horrifying ordeal was over. He was going to see his twelfth birthday after all.

However, instead of slowing down, Dad sped up. Between the Rolls-Royce and **the wall** of police cars was a huge lorry. The lorry's trailer was one that transported cars, though right now it was empty. The lorry driver must have panicked at seeing this car **speeding** straight towards him, as the vehicle spun round dramatically in the middle of the road…

# SCREECH!

…and came to a halt.

Dad seized his chance, and sped towards the back of the lorry. The ramp for loading cars was down. The Rolls-Royce powered on, straight at it.

# BRUM!

It hit the ramp and raced up it. When it reached the top the Rolls-Royce took off and flew through the air.

# WHIZZ!

The boy could feel his heart beating in his chest.
## BOOM! BOOM! BOOM!
It was beating so hard it felt as if it was going to burst out of him. Time slowed down and sped up

all at once. Frank was **flying**. He wanted it to end right now. He never wanted it to end.

The Rolls-Royce soared over the line of police cars, just clipping the roof of one with a back tyre on the way down.

**CRUNCH!**

Before it crash-landed on the road behind the wall of cars with a huge *BUMP!* Frank thought he was going to be hurled into the air as the car bounced down the road like a football.

*BOOM!*
*BOOM!*
*BOOM!*

The boy just managed to grip on to the roof of the Rolls-Royce. In no time, the car righted itself and sped off down the road.

Frank looked over his shoulder to see the chaos his father had caused.

The policemen were struggling to turn their cars round, but as they had stopped in tight formation they had blocked themselves in. The police cars bashed into each other as they attempted to give chase.

*BASH! CRASH! CRUNCH!*

Despite nearly dying a hundred times, the boy couldn't help but smile. His **hero** of a dad had done it again.

# CHAPTER 12

# HURL!

With Frank still clinging to the roof, the Rolls-Royce raced back into the pub car park. Dad must have been in a triumphant mood after his daring jump over the police cars, as he spun the car round backwards into its original parking space, missing the neighbouring vehicles by a centimetre.

## *SCREECH!*

The Rolls-Royce came to such an abrupt halt that Frank couldn't hold on any longer. The force of the stop meant that the boy was instantly catapulted from the roof of the car.

*WHOOSH!*

He soared through the air as if he'd been shot out of a cannon, and he landed in a bush.

"OOF!"

**RUSTLE!**

Fortunately the bush cushioned his fall and no bones were broken.

Although Frank was dazed, he instantly picked himself up and hurried off to find somewhere safe to hide. He didn't want his father to discover he was out late at night in his pyjamas spying on him. If so, the boy would be in BIG trouble.

"WHAT WAS *THAT*?" shouted the man in the passenger seat.

"What was what?" replied one of the men in the back.

"THERE MUST HAVE BEEN SOMEONE ON THE ROOF OF MY MOTOR! AFTER THEM!" shouted the first man.

The two men in the back stumbled out of the car. One was tall and wiry, the other was **big** and **bulky**.

Frank watched from his hiding place behind a bin

in the pub car park. The pair must have been feeling the worse for wear since their stunt drive, as they both looked wobbly. Their faces had turned **green**, and they were bent over, taking shallow breaths.

"I SAID 'AFTER THEM'! What are you waiting for, Fingers?"

"I can't, guv'nor. I think I'm going to hurl," replied the tall, thin one.

"YOU, THEN, THUMBS!"

The bulky one had tears in his eyes. "I wet meself, guv'nor," he murmured. "I can't run in wet underpants."

"WHY NOT?"

"Me mum says I'll get a rash."

"YOU PAIR OF USELESS TWITS!" he shouted. "GILBERT! AFTER THEM!"

Dad climbed out of the car. Since losing his leg, the man walked with a limp. His wooden leg always dragged behind him.

"I am sorry, Mr Big. It's late. I have the babysitter at home. I gotta go."

The little man's eyes narrowed, and his words shot out like bullets. BAM! BAM! BAM! "You are not listening! There was someone on the roof of my Roller. Now the three of you find them. NOW!"

Mr Big might not have been big, but when he snarled it was like coming face to face with a crocodile. Immediately Fingers, Thumbs and Dad all did what they were told. Thumbs waddled awkwardly, as you might well do if you'd wet your pants. The wiry Fingers jabbed Dad in the back, pushing him forward to face whatever danger was lurking in the shadows. Hiding behind the bin, Frank had nowhere to run. He leaned back into the darkness, praying he would not be seen. The three men paced nearer to him. Fingers searched the bushes, skimming the branches with his long, thin digits. Meanwhile Thumbs was **huffing** and **puffing**, getting down on his knees to look under all the cars.

"Nothing here, guv'nor," called out Thumbs.

"Nor here, guv'nor," added Fingers.

Dad was now so near Frank that the boy could hear his father breathing. The man peered behind the bin. Squatting there was his own son, looking guilty and scared and shaken by the ride.

# "IS ANYONE THERE?" shouted Mr Big.

"No. No one," replied Dad, staring his son straight in the eye. "No one at all."

Dad shook his head slightly. The boy took this as a signal to stay as still and quiet as he possibly could. If he moved a muscle, they would both be in

## DEEP TROUBLE.

"It must have been a bird, Mr Big," said Dad.

"Ruddy big bird," muttered the little man. "Now we have to get out of here before the fuzz start sniffing around. Fingers, get the Rolls resprayed and change the number plates in case they trace it."

"Yes, guv'nor."

"Thumbs, you can drive now."

"Thank you, boss," replied the bulky one.

"I want to get home in one piece. Now pile in, all of you."

Dad paced back to the car with his head down, no doubt nervous about giving something away.

"What's going on with you?" hissed Mr Big. The crime boss was as **sharp** as a knife – nothing got past him.

"Nothing."

"I can trust you, can't I?"

"Yes, sir. Absolutely."

"Good. I would hate any harm to come to that boy of yours. Now get in."

From his hiding place, Frank heard the doors to the Rolls-Royce shut.

*CLUNK!*

The car sped off into the night.

A feeling of deep unease descended upon the boy.

His father was mixed up with some **very bad people**.

# CHAPTER 13

## SLAP! SLAP! SLAP!

Frank ran all the way back to his flat. He crouched down at the front door, and looked through the letterbox. It was dark, but he could hear Auntie Flip snoring loudly.

"ZZzz... zzzz... ZZzz... zzzz..."

So the boy quickly opened the door and darted along the corridor to his bedroom. In a hurry, Frank leaped on to his Lilo and burst it.

*BANG!*

**CATASTROPHE!**

The noise woke up Auntie Flip, and she came charging through the door.

"IS EVERYTHING ALL RIGHT?" she bawled. "I HEARD A *BANG!*"

Frank pretended to be asleep.

"ZZZZ... ZZZZ..."

That did not deter Auntie Flip. The lady shouted again, this time right in his ear.

"FRANKIE?"

Still the boy kept his eyes closed.

Now the woman began patting him on the cheeks a bit too hard for Frank to keep pretending to be asleep.

*PAT! PAT! PAT!*

Now the pats became slaps.

*SLAP! SLAP! SLAP!*

Just then Dad entered through the front door, and called out, "Sorry I'm so late, Auntie Flip!"

"That's all right," the boy heard her say. "Frank's been sleeping like a baby all night."

"Has he indeed?" Dad had a hint of surprise in his voice.

"Oh yes. He's been no trouble at all."

"Thank you. I will need you to babysit on Saturday, please."

"It would be a pleasure, Gilbert. I will see you then."

"Thank you, Auntie Flip. Goodnight."

Frank heard the door close, but kept pretending to be asleep. Dad was not fooled. He'd seen his son moments ago hiding behind a bin. Now they had some **serious** talking to do.

# PROMISE

"What on earth did you think you were doing?" demanded Dad as he kneeled on his son's bedroom floor.

"What on earth do *you* think you were doing?" replied Frank.

Dad did not look pleased that his question had been met by a question, and he stood his ground.

"I asked first," said the man.

The boy gulped. He always gulped when he was about to tell a lie. "I couldn't sleep so I just popped out to get some fresh air."

Dad shook his head. "Nice try, mate."

Frank had been **busted**. He had to confess. "All right, Dad – I did follow you. But only because I was worried about you."

"Worried about me? I was worried about you! Hanging on to the roof of a speeding car! *Are you nuts?*"

"It wasn't moving when I climbed on to it," reasoned the boy.

That just made Dad angrier. "You could have got killed!"

This took a moment to sink in. Frank sighed, and replied, "I know, Dad. It was stupid of me. But by the sound of it you are about to do something stupid too."

The man paused. He couldn't be sure how much his son had heard. "It's not what you think it is."

"I think it's something bad."

"It's just driving."

"It can't be just driving. They are **bad** people. Please, Dad. Don't do it."

Now the man had tears in his eyes. "I am trying, OK, mate? I'm trying. I'm trying to do the best for you."

The boy shook his head. "Dad! Whatever it is, I don't want you to do it."

"But it's just one job. That's all. **One job.** Then I'll pay off my debts and still have a bit of money left over for us."

"But, Dad —"

"Please, mate, I know what I'm doing. You saw how I drove tonight."

"I had my eyes closed through a lot of it."

"Well, I can still drive just like the old days."

"I know. But whatever it is they want you to do, please don't. I don't want you to go to prison, or get killed. The accident was bad enough. I'm scared, Dad. *Really scared.*"

Frank wrapped his arms round his father's neck, and pressed his head into his chest. He couldn't help but sob. The sobbing went from son to father in no time. Tears ran down the man's face. He was in a terrible situation. Mr Big and his gang had threatened the person he loved more than anyone else in the whole world – his son. If Dad didn't do what they said, goodness knows what they would do to Frank.

"Come on, mate, don't cry," said Dad as he gently stroked his son's hair like he had since Frank was a baby.

"You've always been my hero, Dad. Please, please, I beg you. Don't do it." The boy lifted his chin and looked into his father's eyes.

The man couldn't bear seeing his son like this.

"Well, if that is how you feel, then I won't do it."

"Really?" asked Frank.

"Really," replied Dad.

A smile crept across the boy's face. "Promise?"

"Promise," replied Dad. "I'll find another way to pay off the money."

"You can always sell my Lilo, Dad," offered the boy. "I don't mind sleeping on the floor."

Somehow this made Dad even **sadder** than before.

"You are such a sweet boy," replied the man, his eyes glistening with tears. "Now give us a **huggle**, and go to sleep."

They wrapped their arms round each other.

"OK, Dad. I will," said the boy.

"Good lad."

With that Dad got up and turned to go. His son called after him.

"Dad?"

"Yep?"

"Whatever happens, you'll always be my hero."

The man said nothing, and closed the bedroom door behind him.

# CHAPTER

## 15

# PSALMS AND PING-PONG

*BRRRING!* went the doorbell.

It was early the next morning, and Frank stumbled down the hallway still half asleep. Looking through the frosted glass in the door, the boy could make out a white flash of dog collar and a larger white flash of teeth. It was Reverend Judith. A word you could use to describe her was *"toothy"*.

The trick with the local vicar was not to let her into your home. If you did let the lady in, nice though she was, you would never be able to get rid of her. Most days the vicar could be found knocking on the doors of the flats, armed with posters she wanted you to put up in your window for jumble sales or cake mornings or Sunday school. Sometimes she would rattle a tin to collect coins for a new church roof, which was in dire need of replacing. Every day the vicar would stuff a new leaflet through the letterbox. She would dream up more and more *bizarre* ways to encourage people to come to church.

**Psalms and ping-pong night**

Come and play ping-pong and read your favourite psalms at the same time. **All welcome. Fridays!**

**ROCK'n' ROLL — with — OUR LORD**

Get on down to the latest rock sounds as you worship! 11am to noon on Tuesdays in the church hall.

**RAP NIGHT**

It's open-mike night on Mondays at 7pm, when any budding rappers can take the mike and rap about anything they like, as long as somehow it involves Our Lord and Saviour.

**Communion-wine tasting**

**Wednesdays at 7pm.**

# Christmas *fancy*-dress roller disco

Get your skates and nativity costume on and celebrate the birth of the baby Jesus as you race around the church hall on wheels. Book for Christmas Eve, Christmas Day or Boxing Day.

# Street-dance competition Thursday night

Whatever your age, come and show Our Lord and Father of all mankind what your crew can do. Freestylin'.

# Crazy golf hymn competition

**Putt as you sing. Tuesday mornings. The winner receives a free hymn book.**

# GRAFFiti is cool!

Come and graffiti the church wall on Saturday evenings!*

* As long as it's white only as the building needs a lick of paint.

# GUNGE YOUR VICAR

On Saturday afternoon I will be locked in medieval-style stocks in the town square, and you are invited to come and throw gunge at me, as long as you swear on your granny's life to come to church on Sunday.

# Drum and bass & cheese afternoon

Dance to your favourite drum & bass tunes while you eat cheese and learn about the path to righteousness. Tuesdays 3pm.

"Lovely to see you again, young Frank," said Reverend Judith with a big toothy grin as Frank opened the front door to her.

"I am sorry I bumped into you!" replied the boy.

"It is I who should be apologising. I bumped into you."

"Sorry."

"Sorry."

"Sorry."

"Sorry. May I come in?" asked the vicar. Her face settled into an expression of a dog begging for a bone.

"In?" asked the boy.

"Yes, in."

"As in... *in here*?"

"Yes, as in *in there*."

"As in *in the flat*?"

"Yes."

"Now?"

"Yes, if it's convenient."

Dad called out from his bedroom. "Who rang the bell?"

"The vicar!" called back Frank.

"Oh no!" replied Dad. "Whatever you do, don't let that blasted woman in!"

Reverend Judith's face dropped. She now looked like a dog that had been abandoned on the side of a road.

Frank attempted a supportive smile. "Dad, she's standing at the door."

"Well, whatever you do, don't open it!"

"It's already open."

There was an awkward silence for a moment.

"Has she heard everything I just said?"

Frank looked to Reverend Judith for confirmation. The lady nodded.

"Yes," replied the boy.

# CHAPTER

# 16

# ALL BAG AND NO TEA

Dad hopped down the hallway in his vest and pants, attaching his wooden leg as he went.

"Reverend Judith!" he announced cheerfully. "What a *lovely* surprise. How *super* to see you! What are you standing at the door for? Come in! Come in!"

"Thank you, thank you. I do like to pop around and see as many of my parishioners as possible," said Reverend Judith as she followed the pair into the kitchen.

"Cup of tea, Vicar?" asked Dad.

"Yes, please. That is very kind. Milk and two sugars."

"Make our guest a cup of tea, will you, mate?"

"Yes, Dad," replied Frank.

Making a cup of tea wasn't an easy task in this household. The kettle had been taken away by the **hard-faced** men, and the family were too poor to afford tea bags or milk.

"So, Vicar, what can we do for you this fine morning?" asked Dad.

"Well, as I'm sure you know, it's Father's Day on Sunday, and I was planning something rather *special* at the church…"

One used tea bag was kept on the side of the sink to be used again and again and again. Now it was looking rather pale, as the tea bag was all bag and no tea.

"…and I wondered if you and your son might like to come up to the front of the church and perform something for the congregation."

Frank was listening to this as he placed the sorry-looking tea bag into a chipped and handle-less mug, and filled it with hot water from the tap.

"What do you mean, 'perform'?" asked Dad, a note of panic in his voice. He hadn't been to church since he was a child, and the thought filled him with **dread**.

"It could be anything, really. Doing a Bible reading, playing the church organ, singing a duet, performing a modern dance piece, reciting a poem."

Frank glanced back at his dad, who had now gone as pale as the tea Frank was making.

"Well, I'm not much of a poet," replied Dad. "My Auntie Flip is the poet in the family."

"**Splendid!**" exclaimed the vicar. "You can read one of hers."

"*What?*" Somehow Dad had agreed to something he'd not agreed to.

Meanwhile, Frank had added some dried-up yoghurt that had been **splattered** on the wall many years ago into the cup for the milk. As for the sugar, the boy had been forced to improvise with a half-chewed toffee that had been stuck to the kitchen floor for some time. He ploPPe^d it in, hoping the lukewarm water would dissolve it.

## It didn't.

With some trepidation, Frank handed the cup of tea (if indeed it could be called that) to the vicar. Reverend Judith peered down into the **horror** the boy had created. It looked like bath water left behind by an ogre. She took a sip. Her nostrils flared, her eyes **watered** and her face went a shocking shade of **green**. Somehow she managed to swallow a mouthful of the **foul** liquid.

Frank smiled to himself. He was rather enjoying this. "More tea, Vicar?"

"Oh bother, is that the time?" announced Reverend Judith, pretending to check her watch, even though she wasn't wearing one.

"I must be going, so I'm sorry I won't be able to finish my delicious tea. I look forward to seeing you both **bright and early** at the church on Sunday morning with your poem!"

Dad nodded his head, and tried to force a smile that just wouldn't come.

As the front door closed, Dad looked down at the worst cup of tea that had ever been made in the history of the world ever.

"Well done, mate – that cup of tea got rid of her."

"What about Sunday morning?" asked Frank.

"What about it?"

"You said you were going to church to read a poem."

### "No, I didn't."

"Well, you never said you *weren't* going to church to read a poem."

### "Well, no, but..."

"No buts. You can't let the vicar down."

### "Why not?"

"Because, because, because… she's a nice lady."

"If she's so nice, why did you try to **poison** the old girl with that tea?" joked Dad.

Frank was annoyed with his father, and didn't want to laugh. But he couldn't help himself.

# "Ha! Ha!"

On seeing his son burst into laughter, Dad shouted, "GOTCHA!"

"I thought those skiddy pants of yours would have been enough to frighten her away!" said Frank.

The man did not look pleased that his underpants, which he'd washed only last month, had been described as skiddy. He sat up to inspect them.

"Whose pants are you calling—? Oh dear."

"Look, Dad. Let's go to church on Sunday. Just this once. It's Father's Day, after all. You aren't doing anything, are you?"

"Sunday morning. No, no, no. No plans."

"Then I better call Auntie Flip, so she can get to work on a special poem for Father's Day."

"Yes. I can't wait," replied Dad in a tone that suggested he'd be more than happy to wait for all **eternity.**

# CHAPTER

## SPLOSH!

There was no telephone in the flat. The line had been cut off years ago because the bill hadn't been paid. Dad was too poor to own a mobile phone, so if they needed to make a call they had to go to a telephone box. The only problem was they didn't have any coins in the house. Fortunately, Frank knew where they could get some.

In the local park stood an old well. People used it as a wishing well, throwing coins down in the hope of a dream coming true. Frank and his father had thrown coins down there many times before. The boy had wished for lots of different things over the years. When he was little, he would wish for toys for his birthday. It was cars mainly, model cars, wind-

up cars, pedal cars, Lego cars, remote-controlled cars.
Once he even wished for his own life-size car. That
was a wish too far. However, since the accident, Frank
only wished for things for his father.

These days Frank and his dad used the wishing
well a little like a bank. They'd put coins in over the
years (a deposit); now they needed to take some out
(a withdrawal). It was just a shame no one ever put
bank notes down. Still, there would be enough money
in there to make a phone call, and if Frank was lucky he
might even have a few coins left over to buy *sweets*.

As father and son entered the park, they saw
that the Rolls-Royce-sized hole
in the fence was being examined
by a bemused-looking park-
keeper.

"Morning!" called out
Dad in his chirpiest voice.

The pair hurried on to
the middle of the park where

the wishing well stood. First they both took a good look around to check that the coast was clear. It was early on Saturday morning, and the town was still waking up, so there weren't many people about. Next Dad unscrewed his leg, and leaned over, upside down, into the well, hooking himself in place with his remaining foot. Frank then clambered down his dad as if he was a climbing frame, and dangled from the wooden leg that Dad gripped tight in his hand. That way they could reach the bottom of the well.

"Are you low enough, mate?" called down Dad. His words echoed in the **blackness**.

"Yes, Dad!"

The boy rolled up his shirtsleeve and skimmed his hand across the bottom of the well. When he was sure he had a large handful of coins, he called, "OK, Dad. I got some. Hoist me up!"

"I am sorry we have to get money this way."

"I don't mind, Dad."

"This is the last time, mate."

"What do you mean?" asked the boy.

But before the man could reply, the pair heard a booming voice shouting down the well.

# "WHAT ON EARTH ARE YOU DOING DOWN THERE?!"

The shock meant Dad lost his grip, and he and the boy tumbled down into the cold water below.

"ARGH!"

S P L O S H !

# CHAPTER

## 18

# DE-TROUSER

"Huh! Huh! Huh!" came the voice from the top of the well.

At the bottom stood Frank and his father, both knee-deep in well-water. Dad knew who it was without looking up. He'd've recognised that snigger anywhere. It was the local policeman, Sergeant Scoff. "Well, well, well. Who have we here?"

The policeman knew exactly who he had here. He'd been making Dad's life a misery for years. Scoff had it in for the man, and was always accusing him of petty crimes on the estate just because he was unemployed.

"Oh, hello, Constable," called up Dad.

"It's *Sergeant!*" bellowed the policeman. His rank was very important to him. Not being the smartest officer on the beat, he'd waited ten long years to progress from constable to sergeant, and he wasn't going to let anyone take that away from him. "Sergeant! Sergeant Scoff! Got it?"

"Yes, Sergeant," replied Dad.

"That's better. Gilbert Goodie! I should have known it was you. The one-legged layabout. The uni-ped idler. The stumpy skiver. Stealing coins from a wishing well now, are we? You couldn't make it up!"

The policeman puffed out his chest, and patted down his hair, which he wore in an outrageous comb-over. Scoff wanted to look his absolute best for the *golden moment* when he got to arrest someone. The man cleared his throat, like an actor about to walk on to a stage. *"I hereby arrest thee for thy crime of coin theft from the aforementioned well of wishes."*

"No," said Dad. "You can't arrest me! That's not what I was doing at all."

"Huh! Huh! Huh!"

There was that irritating laugh again.

"Well, then I would love to know what you are doing down there."

Dad looked to his son. His mind was blank.

"Dad's leg fell off," Frank called up, thinking fast.

"Did it?" whispered Dad.

"Yes. It fell off. We were jogging across the park and Dad's wooden leg just fell off."

The policeman was far from convinced.

"Huh! Huh! Huh! So the leg just fell off, and then, as if by magic, flew through the air and happened to plunge down a well, did it? A likely story! Huh! Huh! Huh!"

The way Sergeant Scoff put it, the story did seem highly unlikely.

"No, of course not," agreed the boy.

"Where are you going with this, mate?" whispered Dad.

"A dog ran off with the leg!" continued Frank. "It must have thought it was a stick. They're both made of wood. And then the dog dropped it down here."

"Did it really?" called the policeman.

"Yes," agreed Dad. "And I hope you can find the owner and give them and that pesky dog a stern ticking-off. Now, for goodness' sake, Sergeant Scoff, please can you help us out of here?"

The policeman sighed wearily, and reached his arm down the well.

Frank climbed on to his father's shoulders, and Sergeant Scoff pulled the boy up. Getting Dad and his leg out was going to be a great deal harder, but the boy had a smart idea.

"Sergeant Scoff, sir?" said Frank.

"Yes, child?"

"We could use your trousers as a rope."

"MY TROUSERS?" thundered the policeman.

"Yes, sir. If you would be kind enough to whip them off, I can lower them down."

"But then everyone in the park would see me in my pants!" the policeman shouted. This was madness!

"If they did, they'd see you as a hero, sir, who rescued a one-legged man from drowning in a well!"

"You might even get a promotion!" shouted up Dad, filling his pockets with coins.

The policeman pondered for a moment. He gazed into the distance, a look of pride on his face. "Will you make me a promise?" asked Sergeant Scoff.

"Yes," replied the boy.

"Will you promise to tell absolutely everyone about this? Get a petition going around the town to award me a *medal of bravery*, and give it to the chief superintendent?"

"You might get a whole chestful!" said the boy.

Without hesitation, the man began unbuttoning his trousers and slipped them off.

"DON'T WORRY, SIR!" shouted the policeman in the hope that people in the park would hear him. *"I, Sergeant Scoff, Will Save Thy Life With The Help Of Mine Own Trousers!"*

Together he and Frank lowered the trousers down the well to pull the man out.

*"There I, A Humble Police Sergeant, Have Saved A Uni-Ped From Certain Death!"* announced the policeman.

"Thank you," said Dad, smiling sideways at his son for persuading this man, who'd made his life a misery, to help them.

Sitting in their wet clothes on the side of the well, Dad began reattaching his wooden leg.

Sergeant Scoff studied the false limb closely, like a master detective. "Mmm. I can't see any bite marks."

"No," replied Frank, thinking fast. "The dog didn't have any teeth."

"A dog with no teeth?" asked the man, incredulous.

"It should make it easier for you to track the animal down," added Dad. "You don't want any more incidents in this town of a dog making off with people's false legs. Could become a crime wave."

"No," replied the policeman. "We certainly don't want any more incidents of canine-based prosthetic-limb theft," he added, a note of sarcasm in his voice.

"If you don't mind, we have a very important date

with a sweet shop," said Dad. "Come along, mate."
The man put his arm round his son's shoulders and
led him off.

After a few steps, the policeman called after them: "I
will be watching you, Gilbert Goodie!"

Without breaking his stride, Dad threw a reply over
his shoulder. "That is nice to know, Constable."

"SERGEANT!" bellowed the policeman,
standing in the middle of the park in his underpants.

Father and son shared a secret smile as they headed
out of the gate. Frank noticed that, apart from his
jingling pockets, Dad also had something stuffed up
his jumper.

"What's that?" asked the boy.

The man lifted his jumper to show the boy.
"Sergeant Scoff's trousers!"

"DAD!" said Frank, bursting into laughter.

"I know, naughty, very naughty!
Now let's make that call to Auntie Flip."

"And get some sweets!"

# CHAPTER 19

# A WARNING

"What did Flip say?" asked Dad. He'd been waiting outside the telephone box in the centre of town as his son made the call.

"What do you think?" replied Frank, rolling his eyes.

"Yes?"

"Yes! Write a poem for church! It was her dream come true. And look," said the boy, unfolding his hand. "We've still got some money left over for sweets."

"You go on ahead. I'll meet you in there," said the man.

The sweet shop was just a few steps up the high street.

Dad seemed restless, as if he needed to be somewhere else.

"Is everything all right, Dad?"

"Yes, mate. I'm fine. Fine. I'll see you at the sweet shop."

With that, the man turned on his heel, and limped off down the road.

"Where are you going, Dad?" the boy called after him.

"Nowhere!"

"You can't be going nowhere. You must be going somewhere…"

Before Frank could finish what he was going to say, his father had disappeared round a corner. The boy shook his head. This was very odd. Even so, he traipsed over to the shop, still dripping water from the well.

*DING!*

The bell on the door dinged as Frank entered Raj's shop, the town's favourite newsagent's. Raj himself was a huge jolly jelly of a man, who probably ate more of his sweets than he ever sold.

"Ah! My favourite but slightly soggy customer! Welcome!" said Raj. To Frank's surprise, the man was down on his knees picking up sweets from the floor, and placing them back on the shelves.

Frank looked around the shop. It was often messy, but it was much messier than normal. In fact, it looked as if a **bomb** had hit it. Magazines were scattered across the floor, pens and pencils had been snapped in half and the freezer had been upturned. Melted ice cream had swirled out of it, forming a multicoloured milky puddle.

"What on earth happened to your shop, Raj?" asked the boy.

"Oh, nothing!" replied the man quickly. "Nothing at all. Don't you worry your little head about it, young sir."

Raj frantically continued trying to put everything back in more or less its rightful place. In the hustle and bustle, a large jar of bonbons was knocked off a shelf and fell on to his head.

## BONK!

The plastic jar broke, showering him in a sugary white dust. Poor Raj slumped down on to the floor in despair.

Frank sat down next to him. He put his arm round the newsagent. "Please tell me, Raj. What happened here?"

"It's these two men. One is **big and fat**, the other is **tall and thin.** They come in to all the local shops and businesses demanding money. If you don't give it to them, they smash the place up. I gave them a hundred pounds, but they said they wanted more next time. Much more. They said they did this as a warning. Next time it would be me they smash up!"

"I think I know who they are. Fingers and Thumbs."

"Yes, that is them!"

"Why don't you call the police about it?"

Raj shook his head sorrowfully. "The men said they will hurt my family if I rat on them. I just don't know what to do!"

"Let me help you tidy up first."

Together the pair did their best to restore some order to the man's shop. Frank glanced at the front pages of some newspapers that had been swept on to the floor. The headlines read:

"I wonder if they were involved in this!" said Raj.

The boy shrugged. "Who knows? There must be some way to stop them!"

"It's a brave person who does. They are bad through and through. They have been **TERRORISING** poor shopkeepers like me all over town for years. I shudder to think what evil they are capable of."

Finally the pair managed to right the freezer. Frank looked on as Raj scooped up the melted ice cream with a rolled-up newspaper.

"Milkshake, young sir? Five p?"

# CHAPTER

## 20

# SEVEN P

"No thanks, Raj," replied Frank.

"No matter." Raj downed the "milkshake" himself. "Mmm, a bit gritty," he mused.

The boy looked at his huge haul of coins from the well. "Raj? What can you buy with seven p?"

Suddenly the newsagent's mood changed, and he smiled broadly.

"Seven p! I have always dreamed of the day someone will walk through that door and spend a whole seven p! I am a rich man!" Raj then looked up to the heavens. "Thank you! There is a God!

Take your time. Browse. My shop is your kingdom..."

Even though Frank was a pauper, Raj always treated him like a *prince*.

"Thank you, Raj. Mmm..." pondered the boy. "I think I'll start with three **BANANA CHEWS**."

"Excellent choice, sir! The healthy option! One of your five a day." Raj looked out of the window. "Ah, there goes your father, Mr Goodie!"

Frank looked up. His father was hurrying down the high street carrying a petrol can.

"Is he not coming in?" said Raj.

"I don't know. Something's not right with him today," said the boy as he watched him go.

A look of panic crossed the newsagent's face. "I know that fudge I gave you last week was a couple of years out of date, but only three people have been admitted to hospital."

"It's not that," replied Frank.

"He was walking funny. I thought like the others his bottom might **explode**."

"No, he walks funny because he only has one leg."

"His leg fell off because he ate my fudge?!" Raj looked to the heavens again and put his hands together in prayer. "Lord, please have mercy on my soul! I am not a bad man. I just use best-before dates as a very rough guide, rounding them up to the nearest decade!"

Frank smiled as he shook his head. He loved Raj like an uncle, a mad old uncle.

"No, no, no, Raj. My dad had a really bad car-racing accident years ago. Remember?"

"Oh yes, yes, of course. I remember. Thank goodness," replied Raj. "Well, not thank goodness. I am just relieved it wasn't my fudge that made him lose a limb."

"Why do parents always keep secrets from their kids?" asked Frank.

The newsagent leaned on his counter, lost in thought. To help give the impression that he was a

deep thinker, he took one of the toy pipes on the shelf, and poPped it into his mouth. The Sherlock Holmes image was shattered when, rather than smoke, soapy **BUBBLES** started to float out of the pipe.

"I suppose mums and dads want to protect their children from stuff. Grown-up stuff that would fill young minds with worry."

"I am grown up!" protested the boy, standing on his tiptoes.

"How old are you?" asked Raj.

"Nearly **twelve**."

"So you are eleven."

"Yes."

Raj shook his head, and blew a huge glistening **BUBBLE** out of his pipe.

The pair smiled at each other, but the moment was interrupted by a deafening sound outside on the street.

# *ROAR!*

The boy knew that sound anywhere.

It was Queenie!

# CHAPTER 21

# BARF

Dad had named his supercharged Mini **"Queenie"** because she was more like a person than a machine. **Queenie** was an old lady, having come off the production line more than fifty years ago. Gilbert would have to coax the car to do what he wanted. The man would talk to her. He would say, "Come on, **Queenie**, wake up," when he was starting the engine. Or if she was low on oil he would say, **"Queenie**, my love, let me buy you a drink." When he was about to give her a wash, he would say, "Time for your bed bath, old girl." Dad loved the car like she was a member of his family. Indeed, when Dad came to in hospital after losing his leg, he was more worried that the car was in bits than that he was.

After the crash, **Queenie** really was in bits. Lots of bits. Mangled bits. Dad might have got a few much-needed pounds for her as **scrap** metal, but he loved the old girl too much for that. So what was left of **Queenie** rusted away in a distant garage on the industrial estate.

Frank loved **Queenie** nearly as much as his father did. The car had a feel, a smell and a sound all her own. It was a sound the boy thought he would never hear again. However, as he stood inside Raj's shop, still choosing how best to spend his seven pence, outside on the road was that sound again.

## *ROAR!*

"**Queenie?**" said the boy, looking around to try to catch sight of her.

"Her Majesty is here in our little town?!" asked Raj. "She must have heard all about my special offer on **Space Dust.**"

"**No! Queenie** is the name of Dad's old racing car!"

Raj nodded. "Yes, of course. That sounded just like her!"

"I know!"

*DING!*

The boy **raced** out of the shop into the street. *Speeding* down the road was indeed a Mini. It was travelling too *fast* for Frank to see who was driving.

It certainly sounded like **Queenie**, but it couldn't be her because the colour was different. **Queenie** was emblazoned with a Union flag that you could spot a mile off. However, instead of being painted red, white and blue, this Mini was a lurid shade of yellow. Dad wouldn't have been seen dead in a car that was the colour of barf.

Raj rushed out of his shop.

"Was it her?" asked the newsagent.

"No. It couldn't have been," replied the boy, downhearted. "It was the wrong colour. Besides, **Queenie** is rusting in some garage somewhere."

"That was one special car."

"I loved her."

"We all did." The newsagent rested a hand on the boy's shoulder. "Don't be sad. Look on the bright side."

"What's that?" asked the boy, looking up at the man.

"You still have a whole *four pence* to spend in my shop!"

Twenty minutes later, Frank still had one mighty p to spend. Buying *sweets* was such a rare treat that he wanted to make it last.

"Mmm, what do I go for, Raj? A pink shrimp?"

"They were caught fresh today."

"Or a flying saucer?"

"They do taste out of this world."

DING!

"Dad!" exclaimed Frank as his father walked into the shop.

"Are you all done, mate?"

"Not quite," replied Frank.

"Still one whole pence left to spend," added Raj.

Dad stalked over to the penny chews. He  picked up the nearest one, a cola bottle, and dropped it in his son's bag.

"I don't like those ones," moaned Frank.

"Don't argue, please. We have to go," snapped Dad. "Thanks, Raj!"

"You know, Mr Goodie, we could have sworn we heard **Queenie** roar down this very street," called out the newsagent.

Dad looked *uncomfortable*. "Really? Well you are wrong."

# CHAPTER

## 22

# TRUST

It was a short walk from Raj's shop back to their flat. As soon as the front door was closed, Dad seemed in a mighty **rush** to get his son to bed. He opened

the last tin of beans, and stood over Frank as he ate it. Then it was time for the boy's "bath", which was a dunk in an oil drum full of water that was **dirtier** than the boy was. He came out a **shade of grey**. Frank used a stained old tea towel to dry himself off. The best part of bedtime was always story-time. They never had books in the house, so Dad would make up stories for his son instead. As the man loved cars, the stories always involved the roar of engines, the smell of burning tyres and speedometers ticking over into red for danger.

"I'm sorry, mate, no story tonight. It's way past your bedtime."

"It's still early, Dad."

"You are tired."

"I am wide awake!"

"You are too old for stories."

"I am only eleven!"

"Nearly twelve."

"Still eleven, though. Come on, Dad. In the time you've spent arguing with me you could have told me a story."

The man sighed. "Once upon a time there was a banger racing car called **Basher. Basher bashed** all the other cars off the track and was the last car standing. The end."

Frank stared at his dad. "Is that it?"

"What do you mean, 'Is that it?'"

"I mean that's not a story!"

"Yes, it is."

"No, it's not."

"Why isn't it a story?"

"It is too short! Once upon a time the end! That's not a story! It was rubbish!"

Dad did not look pleased to be spoken to like this. "Right! Straight to bed!"

"Nooo!"

"Yes! Come on."

Dad put his hands on the boy's shoulders and steered him like a car into his bedroom.

"Put your pyjamas on and get into bed. I mean into Lilo. You know what I mean. Now I need you to be a good boy and go straight to sleep."

Frank looked over to the curtains. They weren't exactly curtains, more bits of cardboard that had been stuck to the window. Round the edges light was shining through. It must still be early.

"What's the time, Dad?"

"I don't know," lied his father.

This seemed very strange to Frank, as his father had been checking his watch all night.

"Well, look at your watch, then, Dad."

"Oh yes," replied Dad. He studied the face for a moment. "The time is bedtime."

## "That's not fair!"

"Auntie Flip will be here any minute. I need you to go to sleep."

"Why is she coming?" demanded Frank.

"I just need to pop out."

## "Where?"

"I am going to watch the banger racing tonight."

"Can I come?"

"No. It goes on too late. Please, mate, I am

begging you. Just go to sleep."

*KNOCK! KNOCK!*

"That will be Auntie Flip. If you don't want her to read you one of her poems, I suggest you go straight to sleep. Now give us a **huggle**, mate."

Dad kneeled down on to his one knee and the pair embraced.

"Dad?"

"Yeah."

"I'm frightened."

"What are you frightened of?"

"I don't know. Something doesn't feel right."

*KNOCK! KNOCK!*

"COMING! Everything will be all right in the morning, mate." The man gave his son a tender kiss on the forehead. "Trust me."

With that, he rose to his foot, and closed the door behind him.

But Frank didn't trust his dad tonight. **Not one bit.**

# CHAPTER

## 23

# SHOPPING TROLLEY

The boy lay still on his deflated Lilo, listening to Dad and Auntie Flip talking in the living room. After a few minutes, Frank's bedroom door opened a little, and Dad peered in. The boy shut his eyes tight in a pantomime of sleep.

"I'm sorry, mate," whispered Dad, "but I have no choice. I have to do this. For both of us."

Frank opened one eye the tiniest bit. He saw his dad framed in the doorway. It was something Frank thought he'd never see again: his father had his old racing gear on. It was a

red, white and blue boiler suit, which he'd not worn since the accident. Now the suit was all **crumpled,** **grimy** and tight on him since his tummy had expanded. Frank knew his father was up to no good. He had to find out what.

The next sound the boy heard was the front door opening.

*CL<sup>UN</sup>K!*

As soon as he heard the front door closing…

*CL<sup>UN</sup>K!*

…the boy leaped up from his Lilo, and made another little dummy of himself in case Auntie Flip poked her head round the door. He pushed his feet into his slippers, in a rush putting the left one on his right foot and the right one on his left. In the living room, Auntie Flip could be heard composing another poem.

*"Looking at you would always make me dotty,*
*Your eyes, your toes, even your little bottom –*

"No... *botty*! This is genius!"

There wasn't time tonight to wait for the lady to go to the toilet. Frank decided he had to create a diversion. He crawled into the kitchen and turned on the tap.

# SPLASH!

He then snuck himself behind the door just as Auntie Flip trundled into the room.

"Most peculiar," said the lady, and she walked over to the sink to turn off the tap. "I hope this place isn't haunted! Ghosts give me the willies!"

Frank seized his moment. He rushed round the kitchen door, ran down the hallway and with the sound of the tap still gushing he opened the front door.

# CLUNK!

The boy closed the door behind him, and peered over the walkway. From up there on the ninety-ninth floor, his father was now a little **dot** moving across the car park below. Frank leaped into his washing basket and flew down the stairs.

*THUD!*

    *THUD!*

        *THUD!*

Just as he reached the bottom he saw his dad limp over to a Rolls-Royce. The last one was white, but this one was silver. Was it the same car? The engine was running and the three men from the other night were

inside. This time Fingers was in the driving seat, with little Mr Big seated next to him. The mighty Thumbs was sitting in the back. He was so heavy that the car was tilting over to one side.

"You're late!" snarled Mr Big.

"Sorry, guv'nor," replied Dad.

"Get in! And you better do what we say or there'll be trouble."

Dad climbed in and the Rolls-Royce roared off.

# BRRMMM!

Frank felt as if he'd been punched hard in the stomach. His dad had lied to him. He was going off to do no good with these bad, bad men. The boy had to stop his father before it was too late, but he had a problem. How on earth was he going to be able to follow a car on foot? He wasn't a fast runner as it was. Frank spotted a discarded shopping trolley upturned on the grass. The boy righted it, and he ran alongside it as if it was a toboggan before leaping in.

# WHIZZ!

By some miracle this shopping trolley was the one shopping trolley in the world that didn't have wonky wheels. It sped along the road, passing an old dear chugging along in her Morris Minor. Frank seized his chance and held on to the side of the car.

**Whizzing** down the road now, the Rolls-Royce was just a few cars ahead.

The traffic lights turned red, and all the cars slowed down to stop. Frank pushed away from the Morris Minor so he could catch up with the Rolls-Royce. So as not to be seen, Frank ducked his head. He grabbed on to the boot handle of the Rolls-Royce just as the light turned **green**. When the car **zoomed** off, so did Frank.

# *BRRMMM!*

Night was falling, and after a few minutes the Rolls-Royce turned off into an industrial estate. The road became bumpy, and the boy was thrown up and down in his trolley.

*CLONK!*
*CLONK!*
*CLONK!*

As he could sense the Rolls was slowing down to stop, Frank let go of the car. Without any brakes, the shopping trolley trundled off at speed. The front wheels hit the pavement, and the trolley did a somersault.

# WHIZZ!

Frank crash-landed

into a hedge.

## DOOSH!

## "OOF!"

The boy was now caged in an upside-down shopping trolley. He pushed it upwards, untangled his pyjamas from the branches of the bush and hid behind a burnt-out old burger van. Frank watched as the four men got out of the Rolls-Royce and looked around. As it was a Saturday night, the industrial estate was empty of people.

Rusty old garage doors squeaked open, and three of the men disappeared inside.

# ROAR!

It was that magical sound again.

Out **zoomed** the yellow Mini, coming to a stop a centimetre from Mr Big's foot.

"Very clever, Gilbert," snarled the crime boss. "So this heap of junk is the getaway car?"

"Trust me, Mr Big," replied Dad. "Her name is **Queenie**. I rebuilt her with my own hands. And she is the greatest racing car in the world!"

# CHAPTER

**24**

# MONSTERS OF THE DEEP

Frank couldn't believe that his father had put **Queenie** back together and not told him. More secrets. More lies. The boy guessed that the coat of yellow paint was to disguise her. **Queenie** was a one-off. A Mini with a Union Jack painted on her would be a dead giveaway to the police.

After a short while, the two henchmen emerged from the garage. Both were holding iron bars and wearing what looked like ladies' tights over their heads. Neither Fingers nor Thumbs were what you might call handsome, but now with their faces all squished down by the tights they looked like **monsters of the deep**.

Frank desperately needed to talk to his father

alone. He had to persuade him to stop this madness. First he needed to create a distraction. Next to Frank's foot was a crushed-up drink can. The boy threw it high in the air, thinking it would land by Mr Big's feet. However, he misjudged his throw, and instead it landed on Mr Big's head.

*BOINK!*

"OW!" screamed the crime boss. "We're under attack!"

This was a much bigger distraction than Frank had intended.

Fingers and Thumbs immediately started rushing around, wielding their iron bars as if going into battle. They whacked everything in sight – bushes, bins, even the burnt-out burger van – in an effort to flush out whoever had hurt their glorious leader.

Frank dashed across the ground on all fours. In the confusion, he managed to scuttle over to the back of the Mini and climbed into the boot. The boy squashed himself inside the small space, and shut the door.

CLICK!

Then he kept as still and quiet as possible so he could listen to what was being said.

"We can't find anyone, guv'nor," began Fingers.

"We've searched everywhere," added Thumbs.

"They have to be hiding here somewhere!" barked Mr Big.

"Maybe it was a rat," guessed Thumbs.

"A rat picked up a drink can and threw it at me?" yelled Mr Big.

"A big rat, guv'nor? One of them super-rats?" suggested Thumbs.

"It landed on my head, you imbecile!"

"The rat could have been riding on the back of a pigeon!"

"Just go!" yelled Mr Big. "And bring me back the booty. Or there will be trouble."

"Right you are, guv'nor," replied Fingers.

The door of the Mini opened and closed, and Frank could feel the car sink a little as the two henchmen got inside.

# ROAR!

The car's engine *revved* up, and the back wheels screeched. Then she *lurched* forward at terrific speed. Frank was immediately slammed against the door of the boot...

# "OOF!"

...as **Queenie** raced off into the night.

# CHAPTER 25

# BOOM!

*R*O*A*R*!*

Frank was thrown around like a sack of potatoes in the boot as **Queenie** raced down the roads. Finally the little car came to a halt.

*SCREECH!*

Somehow the boy was still alive, though he had absolutely no idea where they were. All he did know was that his father was driving a getaway car, but what they were getting away from was a mystery. The boy put his ear next to the boot door, and listened.

First the car door opened.

*CLICK!*

Then there was the sound of footsteps.

*TAP. TAP. TAP.*

Soon after there **BOOM!** was an explosion.

An alarm sounded.
*RING!*

Then he heard Fingers shouting. "Come on! We have five minutes until the police arrive."

The boy had to see what was going on.

He forced open the boot a tiny bit...

C*LICK*.

...and peeked out.

There was black smoke from the explosion, but as it cleared Frank could make out a sign that read:

**BANK.**

The boy was only eleven (nearly twelve) but he had found himself in the middle of a real-life bank robbery. Suddenly he was scared, not just for himself but also for his dad. If the police caught his father, he'd be sent to prison for a very long time. Frank leaped out of the boot, and crawled along the road beside the car. He poPpe_d his head up at the driver's window.

"Argh!" cried his dad upon seeing his son. He wound down the window. "What are you doing here?" the man demanded.

"What are *you* doing here?" the boy demanded.

"I asked first!" snapped Dad.

"I was worried. I climbed in the boot. I didn't want you to do anything stupid."

"What's more stupid than climbing into the boot of a car?"

"Robbing a bank?" said the boy.

"We are not robbing a bank," replied Dad.

"What are you doing, then?"

"Fingers and Thumbs are just checking their savings accounts."

"By blowing the door off?"

"It's Saturday night. They didn't realise the bank was closed."

Frank rolled his eyes. "Look, Dad, I may be a kid, but I'm not daft. I know exactly what you are doing. Now you need to get us out of here. *Fast.*"

"I can't," replied Dad.

"Why not?"

"They are bad men, Frank. They are capable

of bad things. They'll hurt me. They'll hurt you."

"Then let's just drive and drive and drive and never stop!"

"They'll find us!"

At that moment Fingers and Thumbs ran out of the bank carrying a brown suitcase, which wasn't quite shut. It was trailing money. Fifty-pound notes were fluttering in the sky like butterflies.

# "DRIVE!" shouted Thumbs.

On seeing this child standing by the car, Fingers shouted, "What the blazes is the kid doin' 'ere?"

"I don't know him," said Dad. "Hey, kid, scram!"

Fingers looked at the boy. "He looks just like you."

"Poor boy," replied Dad.

"He is your son!"

Dad looked at Frank again. "Oh yeah, so he is."

"So what is he doin' 'ere?" demanded Thumbs.

"I thought it was bring-your-kid-to-work day," replied Dad, clearly hoping a joke might soften them. He was wrong, as the two goons gave the man a death stare.

# NEE-NAW! NEE-NAW!

There wasn't time to explain as a police car was speeding down the road towards them.

"It's the fuzz," yelled Fingers. "Come on!"

Fingers and Thumbs dived into the Mini through the passenger side.

"MATE! GET IN!" shouted Dad as he revved the engine.

"How?" pleaded the boy.

"JUMP!"

The police car sped closer and closer.

*NEE-NAW! NEE-NAW!*

Dad revved the engine.

*ROAR!*

The two heavies in the back started shouting.

"LEAVE THE FOOL!"

"NASTY LITTLE RUNT!"

"MATE! JUMP IN!" begged Dad.

With that, the boy leaped head first into the car. The engine roared and **Queenie** sped off down the street, with Frank's bottom sticking out of the window.

# CHAPTER 26

# HOT PURSUIT

Never stick your bottom out of a car window.

If you *have* to stick your bottom out of a car window for whatever reason, make sure you are wearing something warmer than pyjamas. That is because there is a very real danger you will develop a condition called **"bottom freeze"**. This is when a person's bottom temperature descends to danger levels. Bottoms can get so cold they actually turn blue. In very serious cases, frozen bottoms have been known to **crack** or even <sup>snap</sup> off.

**Bottom freeze** can be brought on in a number of ways...

doing a number two in an igloo...

sticking your bottom in a freezer...

trying to melt a snowman using only the heat from your naked bottom...

attempting to catch a polar bear in the Arctic using your bottom as bait...

tobogganing on your bare bottom...*

* Tobottoming

accidentally sitting on an icicle... (That can be painful too, if the icicle is sharp.)

cryogenically freezing your bottom so it will live on for future generations...

mistaking an iceberg for a nice comfy sofa...

becoming trapped under an out-of-control Mr Whippy machine...

Frank's bottom was becoming dangerously cold as **Queenie flew** through the town with the police car in hot pursuit. Dad pulled his son into the car, and the boy **shuffled** across his father's lap, before **crawling** into the back seat next to Thumbs.

The gorilla of a man **stared** at the small boy.

"Good evening," said Frank, not sure what to say to this brute.

"No, it isn't," replied the big man.

Thumbs looked out through the back window.

The one police car had become three. They were gaining on them.

# *NEE-NAW! NEE-NAW!*

"Throw the boy out," ordered Thumbs. "He's slowing us down."

"In fairness, I think you might weigh a **tiny** bit more," said the boy.

If this was designed to lighten the mood, it backfired badly.

## "Are you calling me fat?" growled Thumbs.

"No, but you do weigh more."

"Stop bickering in the back," ordered Fingers.

"He started it!" replied Thumbs. "He's picking on me for my size."

"Shut up and hold tight!" said Dad as they **whizzed** round a corner.

They had now reached the outskirts of town.

"Where on earth are you going?" demanded Fingers. "This isn't the way to the guv'nor's mansion."

"I know. I thought we could take a little shortcut."

Dad turned the steering wheel sharply, and the car started going up some **steep** steps.

# BONK!

# BONK! BONK!

"Where are you taking us?" shouted Fingers as his long fingers gripped on to his chair.

"We are going to lose them," said Dad.
**Queenie** *crashed* through a barrier, and suddenly
they were on the pitch of a football ground. The three
police cars were still in hot pursuit.

# *NEE-NAW! NEE-NAW!*

The Mini came to a halt in the dead centre of the pitch. The three police cars **fanned** out and stopped too.

A voice came over a loudspeaker on top of one of the police cars.

**"THIS IS** Sergeant Scoff.**"**

"He must want his trousers back," said Frank.

"GIVE YOURSELVES UP. WE HAVE YOU SURROUNDED."

"Who fancies a game of football?" announced Dad.

## CHAPTER
## 27

# GOAL!

"Sounds good, Dad!" replied Frank.

*ROAR!*

**Queenie** sped off up the steps into the stand where the spectators sit.

*BONK!*

*BONK!*

*BONK!*

One of the police cars gave chase.

*BONK!*

*BONK!*

*BONK!*

"Shift over!" shouted Dad to Thumbs.

The henchman did what he was told and slid over to Frank's side of the car.

Then Dad turned the steering wheel sharply and put the Mini on to two wheels. It just fitted through the gangway between the rows of seats. Frank was squashed by having this man-mountain on top of him, but didn't feel this was the right moment to complain. The police car giving chase behind ploughed through the seats.

NEE-*NAW! NEE-NAW!*
*THWACK! THWACK!*
*THWACK!*

The seats flew up into the air, and smashed into the windscreen of the police car. The driver could not have been able to see where he was going, because the police car smashed straight into the giant TV screen.

CRASH!

The police car dangled out of the screen, like a film in 3-D.

"One down, two to go," said Dad.

He turned the steering wheel sharply and **Queenie**

went up on to two wheels again, and bumped down

the stairs…

# BONK!
# BONK!
# BONK!

…on to

the pitch.

The two remaining police cars were waiting on the far side. They surged forward towards the Mini at terrific speed, tearing up the grass.

The Mini **surged** forward too.

The cars were hurtling towards each other across the pitch.

**This was a dangerous game of chicken.**

Who would crumble first?

"**Argh!**" screamed Fingers. He closed his eyes as the police cars headed straight for them.

"Make it stop!" bawled Thumbs. Frank looked at the beast of a man, who was close to tears.

If someone didn't slam on the brakes, there would be a head-on collision.

Dad held his nerve.

He was a champion banger racer, after all. Waiting until he could see the whites of the policemen's eyes he yanked on the handbrake and spun the car round **wildly** on the spot.

"NOOO!" cried Fingers and Thumbs.

The two police cars turned sharply. One turned too sharply and ended up on its roof, skidding across the pitch.

Dad expertly took the Mini out of its spin and nudged the upside-down police car into the back of the net.

"GOAL!" shouted Frank.

Now there was just one police car standing.

# 28

# A MIGHTY DUEL

**Queenie** sped around the pitch and the police car chased her on the inside. They did lap after lap after lap. Round and round they raced. It was like the last two cars left in a banger race.

Frank saw that one of the officers in the police car was Sergeant Scoff. The policeman had a wild look in his eye and was leaning out of the window, his comb-over flapping in the breeze. He was shouting orders to the officer driving the car.

*"FASTER! FASTER! GO! GO!"*

Scoff stared into the Mini. The two robbers had their faces squashed by ladies' tights, but Frank and his father didn't have any form of disguise. The boy panicked. Would Sergeant Scoff recognise him and Dad?

*THUNK!*

Dad bashed the Mini into the police car and sent it spinning towards the goal.

Somehow the police officer driving managed to regain control of the car and stopped just short of the goal line.

# SCREECH!

Dad put his foot down on the accelerator and powered straight towards the police car.

The bonnets of the two cars bashed.

# CLUNK!

It was like two buffalo locking their heads together in battle.

Engines thundered.

# ROAR!

Wheels spun. *WHIZZ!*

Metal crunched.

# CRUNCH!

This was a **mighty** duel.

All of a sudden it seemed as if Dad was losing. The police car was surging forward, pushing the Mini backwards. Frank looked up at the policemen staring in at them. Their faces were lit up with glee. They were winning. Or so they thought.

"WHAT ARE YOU DOING, GILBERT?" shouted Fingers.

"THEY'VE GOT US, YOU IDIOT!" yelled Thumbs.

"Or have they?" said Dad.

In a flash, he threw the Mini into reverse.

Frank looked out of the rear window.

Now they were going backwards towards the goal.
The police car *accelerated.* Just at the last moment
Dad turned the steering wheel of the Mini sharply,
and the car **spun round**.

The police officer driving was taken by surprise
and his car ploughed straight past them into the goal.

SMASH!

"GOAL!" shouted Frank.

"Now let's get out of here!" said Dad.

The car sped off towards the gate.

Father and son cheered as the car bounced down the steps.

BONK! BONK! BONK!

But they weren't safe yet. Just as they reached the road, they saw a semicircle of police cars ahead. Dad threw the car into reverse, but it was too late. More police cars came from behind, and stopped in formation, bumper to bumper. The Mini was now trapped in a circular cage of police cars.

A police helicopter hovered
overhead, shining a spotlight
on the Mini.
**There was no way out.**

# CHAPTER

## 29

# NO WAY OUT

"GIVE YOURSELVES UP!
WE HAVE YOU SURROUNDED!"

came a voice over a loud-hailer.

It was Scoff, standing at the top of the steps that led into the football stadium. The policeman looked a little dazed after his car had so spectacularly hit the back of the net, but at least he'd found another pair of trousers, even though this pair was too short for him. His outrageous comb-over was whipping up into the air as the helicopter's blades spun. The mini-tornado it was creating threw leaves and litter spinning into the air all around the Mini. The little car rattled so hard it sounded as if it was going to fall apart.

*RITTLE! RATTLE! RUTTLE!*

Dad gulped. Even the hardened criminals Fingers and Thumbs were looking worried.

Frank had watched his father race for years. He'd marvelled as the champion banger racer manoeuvred himself out of the most impossible situations. There must be *some* way to escape.

"Dad, you can drive us out of anything," urged Frank.

"It's too dangerous, mate. We need to give ourselves up. This is the end."

"It's all this little runt's fault for slowing us down," snarled Fingers.

"I want to rip his head off and use it as a football!" growled Thumbs.

Despite becoming distracted by the unsavoury thought of his head being detached from his body, the boy was determined that they'd escape. Many years ago he'd seen his father do a terrific stunt in **Queenie** when he'd flipped the car on to its back wheels.

"Dad, you can jump those police cars!"

"No, I can't!" replied the man.

"You can! Do a **Queenie** wheelie!"

"A WOT?" demanded Thumbs.

"You can't do a wheelie in a car," sneered Fingers.

"My dad can!"

"Not now he can't," replied Dad. "When I did that stunt, **Queenie** was specially weighted. I had this huge **heavy** barrel in the back."

"You've got a huge **heavy** barrel in the back now," replied Frank, nodding towards Thumbs.

The henchman leaned into the boy. It looked for a moment as if he might eat him.

"That's not enough, mate. All three of us grown-ups would have to squeeze in the back."

"What are you waiting for?" exclaimed the boy.

"Who's gonna drive?" asked Dad.

"ME!" replied Frank.

# CHAPTER

30

## COUNTDOWN

"YE HAVE TEN SECONDS OR I DOTH USE CONSIDERABLE FORCE!" announced Sergeant Scoff over the loud-hailer. He spun his truncheon round in his hand, looking eager to use it.

"You can't drive!" said Fingers mockingly. "What are you? Ten?"

"I'm nearly twelve! Now do what I say if you want to get out of here!"

**"TEN!"** came the voice.

"All of you bundle in the back!"

Fingers and Dad looked reluctant, but did what the boy said.

**"NINE!"**

As the pair scrambled into the back, the boy scrambled into the front.

**"EIGHT!"**

"Budge up!" shouted Fingers to Thumbs as he squeezed himself on to the back seat.

"I can't budge up," moaned Thumbs. "I can't help it if I have a big bottom."

**"SEVEN!"**

With the three men all in the back and the boy in the front, the front of the Mini began to rise.

**"SIX!"**

Frank couldn't hide his smile. In spite of all the danger, he was now sitting in the driving seat of **Queenie**, something he had waited his whole life to do.

**"FIVE!"**

The boy put his hands on the steering wheel. He'd never felt so cool.

**"FOUR!"**

He reached his feet down to the pedals.

DISASTER!

His legs were too short!

"DAD! I CAN'T REACH THE PEDALS!" shouted the boy.

**"THREE!"**

"I AM GOING TO THROTTLE HIM!"

shouted Fingers.

"AND WHEN YOU HAVE FINISHED
THROTTLING HIM I AM GOING TO
THROTTLE HIM SOME MORE!"
added Thumbs.

## "TWO!"

They had one second to go.

# 31

# DEMOLITION DERBY

"Here, mate!" cried Dad. "Use this!"

The man pulled off his wooden leg and passed it to the boy.

## "ONE!"

As quickly as he could, the boy hooked his foot into the elastic strap at the top.

## "RIGHT! CHARGE!" announced

Sergeant Scoff. He began running down the steps, waving his truncheon. A one-man crusade.

The boy put his foot down on the wooden leg, which pressed the accelerator pedal.

The Mini *roared* forward. With its front wheels off the ground, the car mounted the bonnet of one of the police cars.

CRUNCH!

The Mini crushed the bonnet.

DUNK!

The back wheels of the Mini rolled over the police car's windscreen.

SMASH!

"SPIN THE WHEEL LEFT!" shouted Dad.

Frank did what his father said, and the car started driving over the next police car in the circle. All the police officers leaped out of their cars just in time.

"NOW EVERYONE LEAN FORWARD!" shouted Dad, and all three men in the back threw their weight *frontwards*.

The Mini then slammed down on to four wheels.

BASH!

Frank drove over the top of the next police car. And the next. And the next.

**CRUNCH!**

As the Mini **zoomed** over them, it left a trail of destruction. The glass in all the windscreens exploded as the Mini's wheels rolled over the cars.

**BOOM! BOOM! BOOM!**

CRUNCH!

CRUNCH!

And the weight of **Queenie** crushed the police cars' roofs.

Frank had only once been in trouble at school – for sneezing loudly in class. Now he was his very own **DEMOLITION DERBY!**

Scoff looked on in horror as the whole fleet of police cars was turned into scrap metal.

As soon as Frank had completed his lap, his dad shouted, **"HARD RIGHT!"** The Mini rolled down the back of a police car and landed on the ground with a loud…

*BUMP!*

Sparks flew as the bumper scraped the tarmac.

# FIZZLE!

Then the Mini flew down the open road.

*WHIZZ!*

**"WHOO HOO!"** screamed the boy. Frank had never to his knowledge screamed "whoo hoo!" before, but this seemed like the perfect time.

Dad looked on as the speedometer was nudging out of its range. The car was going well over one hundred miles an hour.

Overhead, the police helicopter was giving chase.

*WHIRR!*

"We're not out of the woods yet," said Dad. "Let me take over now, mate. I can outsmart that chopper!"

"Of course, Dad."

The boy tried to move the wooden leg over to the brake pedal, but it had become jammed on to the accelerator.

"DAD!"

"What, mate?"

"I CAN'T STOP THE CAR!"

# CHAPTER 32

# WHAT GOES UP MUST COME DOWN

The excitement immediately turned to terror as Frank realised they were heading to their doom. With Dad's false leg stuck on the accelerator pedal, **Queenie** was going faster and faster and faster.

"HOLD ON, MATE!" said Dad as he clambered over the back seat into the front.

As he did so, his stump bashed Fingers's long, pointy nose.

"Watch what you are doing with that thing!" snapped Fingers.

"Sorry!" called out Dad.

He wiggled this way and that to heave himself forward.

Frank swerved the car as it went round a

roundabout faster than lightning.

This caused Dad to tumble back. His bottom squashed right into Fingers's face.

"EURGH! WATCH WHAT YOU ARE DOING WITH THAT THING!" shouted the henchman.

"SORRY!" called out Dad as he thrust his bottom back on to the man's nose so he could launch himself forward into the passenger seat. "OOF!" he cried, sliding down into the front of the Mini. Still the car just kept going faster and faster and faster. Frank was clinging on to the steering wheel, staring forward into the dark road ahead of him. He didn't dare blink. Now they'd reached the countryside. There were no streetlights – it was that real country darkness. The road had narrowed into a single lane with high hedgerows on each side. If there was a car coming the other way, they would all be done for.

Overhead they could hear the police helicopter still following them. *WHIRR!*

"Kill the lights!" ordered Dad.

The boy flicked a switch and the car's headlights were turned off. Now no one could see them, and they couldn't see anything, either.

Soon the sound of the helicopter overhead became fainter.

# "I THINK WE'VE LOST THEM! NOW, FOR THE LAST TIME, STOP THE CAR!" shouted Fingers.

"I'm trying!" replied Dad, and he bashed at his own wooden leg with his fist. But it just wouldn't budge.

Way ahead in the distance the boy could make out something on the road. Something pink. Something fat. Something piggy.

It was a pig!

"PIG!" shouted Frank, not sure what else to say on seeing a pig.

"How dare you!" cried Thumbs.

It must have escaped from one of the farms by eating its way through the hedge. Perhaps the sound of the helicopter whirring overhead had startled it.

"No. Not you! There's a pig on the road!"

"RUN IT OVER!" said Fingers.

"I CAN'T KILL A PIG!" shouted the boy.

"You eat pork, don't you?" yelled Fingers.

"Yes."

"Well then, you can run over a pig!"

Thumbs looked bemused. "Fingers? Does pork come from a pig?"

"YES!" shouted Fingers.

"Oh, you learn something new every day!"

"I've done it!" said Dad as he whacked the wooden leg off the accelerator pedal. He then scrambled down into the footwell, and thumped the brake pedal as hard as he could.

# SCREECH!

It was too hard.

The car's back wheels shot up and the Mini somersaulted through the air.

## WHUF! WHUF! WHUF!

"ARGH!" screamed everyone as they flew for what seemed like minutes but must have been seconds. Through the windscreen Frank looked down and stared into the pig's eyes. Both his eyes and the pig's were wide open with horror.

"OINK!"

The car was flying upside down through the air. Of course, what goes up must come down.

The car skimmed over a hedge.

*SKISH!*

Before landing in a field on its roof.

*BASH!*

All four passengers were dangling upside down as the car skidded backwards across a field full of cattle.

*WHUZZ!*

The cows were all lying down asleep, until the sight of an upside-down Mini speeding along the wet grass rudely woke them up.

"MOO! MOO!" mooed the cows as they desperately clambered up to get out of the way.

All four inside the car stared out of the back windscreen. A tall tree was fast approaching.

"TREE!" shouted Thumbs.

"Yes, we've seen it!" said Fingers.

"Slam the brakes!" shouted Thumbs.

**"We're upside down!"** said Dad.
**"Oh yeah!"** replied Thumbs.

# SULK

"HOLD TIGHT!" shouted Frank as he realised they were half a second from impact.

# CRUNCH!

The back end of the car crashed into the tree, and **Queenie** came to an abrupt halt.

Dazed and confused, the four hung upside down for a moment before scrambling out of the car.

As Frank lay on his back in the grass, he could feel something rough and slobbery licking his forehead. Looking up, he saw that it was a huge cow's tongue. The herd had gathered around the upturned car, and were now licking the people back to life.

"MOO! MOO!"

"Get off me!" shouted Fingers, pushing the cow's

face away, which only seemed to make the animal want to lick him more.

"So what meat comes from these things?" asked Thumbs innocently. "Is it chicken?"

Fingers sighed loudly.

"I need everyone's help now!" announced Dad.

"Lamb?" guessed Thumbs.

"Listen! We all need to work together to roll the car back up the right way. Now, Frank, you and I can take this end, and Fingers and Thumbs—"

But before Dad could finish giving his orders, Thumbs pulled the car up and righted it without any help. It landed on the grass with a *THUD*.

"Oh, thank you, Thumbs," said Dad. "You seem to have done it all on your own."

"Right!" snapped Fingers.

"After you two nearly killed us, I'm going to drive from now on."

"I never get to drive!" huffed Thumbs.

"Well, I bagsied it first!" snapped Fingers.

"I will drive!" announced Dad.

"NOT FAIR!" grumbled both Fingers and Thumbs.

Dad reattached his wooden leg, and got into the driver's seat. "Look, *I'm* the getaway driver so *I'm* going to drive."

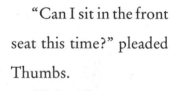

"Can I sit in the front seat this time?" pleaded Thumbs.

"No!" said Dad.

"Can I sit in the front seat this time?" pleaded Fingers.

"NO!"

"WHY NOT?" the two henchmen asked.

"Because if I let one of you sit in the front seat then the other one in the back will moan and then I will have to stop the car again so you can swap. It will all take too long."

"Let's get a move on, then. We need to be at Mr Big's house by midnight," said Thumbs.

Fingers whacked Thumbs round the back of the head.

"Ow! What was that for?" whined the big man.

"Don't tell the kid where we're going. It's top secret."

"Mr Big's house?" asked Thumbs.

Fingers whacked him again, harder this time.

"Ow! I never told him that Mr Big masterminded the robbery!"

Another whack.

"OOOWWW!!!"

"Stop it! The pair of you. Or you will both have to walk!" said Dad.

Both men got into the back seat and began to sulk.

No one likes being told off, especially not hardened criminals.

Frank slid into the front seat. The boy was enjoying all this greatly. "Don't worry. I didn't hear that we are going to Mr Big's house or that he masterminded this and all your other robberies," he said with a smirk.

"That's good!" said Thumbs. "See?"

Fingers shook his head.

"**Quiet, everyone!**" said Dad as he tried desperately to start the car.

*GRRR... GRRR... GRRR...*

Instead of shuddering into life, **Queenie** let out a low, grinding noise.

"Oh no," said Dad.

"What?" asked the boy.

"The engine must have flooded when she went upside down. The poor old girl won't start again now for hours. We're going to have to walk."

"Maybe we should call the police?" suggested Thumbs. "See if they can tow us."

"We're escaping from the police, remember!" shouted Fingers.

"Oh yeah."

"See what I have to deal with?" said Fingers to anyone who would listen.

"Come on," said Dad. "The sooner we start, the sooner we'll get there."

At that moment a bolt of lightning lit up the sky.

# CRACKLE!

After a few seconds, a roll of thunder could be heard and rain poured down from the skies.

# B°°M!
## TAT! TAT! TAT!

"I think it's raining," observed Thumbs.

Fingers picked up the brown suitcase stuffed with cash. He threw it at Thumbs a little too hard.

"OW!" cried the henchman.

"You can carry it! Come on! This way!" announced Fingers, and the four began the long march to Mr Big's house.

Dad and Frank took a last look back at poor **Queenie**. The rain was pouring down, and the yellow paint was running off on to the field, revealing the Union Jack underneath.

"What about **Queenie**?" asked Frank.

"We'll come back for her, mate," said Dad. "Don't you worry."

# CHAPTER

# 34

# CRIME DOES PAY

After trudging across fields covered in cowpats in the pouring rain, the group arrived at a set of huge iron gates. A sign outside read "Pilfer House".

"This is it!" said Fingers. He pressed a buzzer, and leaned into an intercom.

"Mr Big residence?" came a voice from the speaker.

"It's Fingers and Thumbs. We've got a present for the guv'nor," said Fingers.

"He's been expecting you. One moment, please."

Slowly the gates whirred open and the four walked up the long driveway. At the end of it was an enormous country house. In all his eleven years, Frank had never seen a home so grand. It looked like *a palace* with its thick Roman-style columns, tall windows and stone

steps leading up to a huge wooden door.

Looking at all this in awe, Frank muttered, "Crime does pay."

They passed an ornamental fountain, which had at its centre a giant marble statue. It was a likeness of Mr Big himself, striking a heroic pose with his dressing gown flying in the wind like a cape. He'd made himself look like a **superhero**, rather than the **supervillain** that he really was.

The four climbed the stone steps to the imposing wooden door. Fingers knocked with the solid gold knocker. *BOOF! BOOF! BOOF!*

After a few moments a butler in a bow tie and tails answered the door.

"My master is waiting in the study for you," he announced. He was a short, thin man with an unsmiling face. From his accent and appearance, Frank could tell he was Chinese.

The butler led them down a long corridor, and into Mr Big's study.

"You're late!" snarled Mr Big. The little man was seated behind a large desk in his office, chomping on a cigar. At his feet were two fat black cats, with diamond-encrusted collars. The room was an embarrassment of gold. *Gold desk, gold chair, gold lamps, gold frames* around *gold paintings* of Mr Big wearing *gold.* One even depicted Mr Big as a Roman emperor with a *crown of gold leaves* on his head. This was a man who loved *gold* nearly as much as he loved himself.

"Sorry, guv'nor," said Fingers. "We 'ad a little problem with the getaway car."

The henchman shot a look to Dad, who bowed his head.

"And who is this *little worm?*" demanded Big.

"My son, sir," replied Dad.

"Oh, so I finally meet the little squirt. Your mum has told me a bit about you."

"My mum?" said the boy, trembling.

"Didn't your daddy tell you?" said Mr Big with a smirk. "She's *my* woman now."

Frank looked back to his father, desperately confused. "Dad? Please tell me this isn't true!"

The man took a deep breath. He'd protected his son from the truth for so long. Now he had no choice but to tell him the whole story.

"I am so sorry, son. It is true. Your mother lives here with Mr Big."

Immediately Frank felt as if he was underwater. The world around him felt silent and heavy. He couldn't think. He couldn't speak. He couldn't breathe.

Dad wrapped his arms round his son. "I should have told you, mate, but I wanted to protect you from the truth."

Frank didn't want to cry in front of these men. He wanted to be strong. But he couldn't. Through tears he asked, "Please don't tell me my mum is here right now in this house."

Mr Big smiled. "Of course she is! I don't let her out!"

The two henchmen laughed at this joke, which, like most jokes, was serious.

"Ha! Ha!"

"Yes, Mummy's here," continued Mr Big. "Around this time of night you can find her alone in the drawing room downing a bottle of vintage champagne. Something your daddy here could never provide for her."

The henchmen laughed again: "Ha! Ha!"

"So, little Frankie," began Mr Big, "do you miss your mummy? Do you want to see her?"

"No!" snapped the boy.

"Well, I bet she wants to see you. It's been a while. Chang, tell the lady of the house her son's here."

"Yes, master," said the butler, bowing as he left the room.

Dad put a protective arm round his son. "Don't do this to the boy," he demanded.

"I can't wait to see this!" replied Big. "Mother and son reunited at last!"

"I don't want to see her, Dad," sniffed the boy.

"Come on, mate. Let's get out of here," said Dad, taking his son by the hand.

But it was too late. The boy's mother appeared in the doorway.

# 35

# CHAMPAGNE, PERFUME AND HAIRSPRAY

Mum looked very different to how Frank had remembered her. Now she was all hair and make-up and nails. Her skin was a good shade darker, and she was *dripping in gold jewellery*. She looked like a gangster's moll, which was exactly what she had become.

"Oh, haven't you grown?" slurred the woman, holding a glass of champagne with lipstick smudged round the rim.

Seeing her after all this time seemed unreal to the boy. Eventually Frank managed a "Hello, Mum."

Mr Big beamed. He seemed to be enjoying all this. "Ain't you gonna give your mummy a kiss?"

The boy shook his head.

"Come on, Frankie!" she said as she stumbled into the room. The woman tottered on her too-high heels, like a foal taking its first steps. Eventually she was nose to nose with her son. The boy had to close his mouth and try not to breathe, such was the stench of champagne, hairspray and perfume. "NOW GIVE ME A KISS!" she demanded.

"I don't want to!" said the boy.

"You rude little toerag!" she snarled.

Fingers and Thumbs looked on, smirking at the scene. The two black cats purred.

Dad leaped in. "You leave my son alone!"

The woman turned her head slowly towards him. When her eyes met his, she said, "Gilbert, you are forgetting something. Frank is *my* son and all."

The boy felt caught in the middle. Somewhere deep inside him, he still *loved* his mother, even though she'd let him down so badly over the years.

"Please don't do this," pleaded Dad. "Not now."

The boy wrapped his arms round his father's chest and held on tight.

The woman's face glowed with anger. "I am going to bed!" she huffed.

"No, no, no," ordered Mr Big. "Stay here, my love. I want you to see what these nice gentlemen have brought me."

Chang nodded to Fingers and Thumbs. The pair snapped into action and emptied the brown suitcase full of money on to the desk. There were bundles and bundles of fifty-pound notes.

Each bundle looked like a hundred notes, and there were at least a hundred bundles.

So that was 50 x 100 x 100. Maths wasn't Frank's strong subject – all he knew was that that was a lot of noughts.

"Look at it, woman!" said Mr Big.

Mum's eyes lit up. "Oh, Biggie! It's beautiful!"

The little crime boss scooped up huge bundles of cash and handed them to her. "There you go, babes. Buy yourself something nice for your birthday."

"You're the best, Biggie!" squealed Mum as she threw her arms round Mr Big and gave him a long, **slobbering kiss.**

## *SLURP!*

Frank and Dad looked away, and even Fingers, Thumbs and Chang stared at the ceiling.

"Don't be long!" she purred as she poured the last of the champagne down her throat and wobbled on her high heels.

The woman plucked a
bundle of notes from one
of her wads, and stuffed
it in the top pocket
of the boy's pyjamas.
"Here's some pocket
money."

"I don't want your
money," replied Frank, and
he took the notes out and stuffed them back in her
hand.

"What do you want, then?" slurred the woman.

"I don't want anything from you," said Frank. "I
don't want to see you ever again!"

The woman's face darkened. It was as if she'd
transformed into a serpent. Mum raised her hand as if
she was going to slap her son across the face…

# CHAPTER 36

# LOOT

Dad reached out and grabbed Mum's wrist to stop her. He held on to it tightly, a millimetre from Frank's face.

"What are you doing, Rita?" asked Dad.

"I don't know, Gilbert!" replied the woman, suddenly shocked by what she might have done.

"Haven't you hurt our boy enough already?"

"I know. I'm sorry. I am so sorry. I don't know what came over me," she spluttered, tears running down her cheeks. "I've let you down, Frank. That's all I've ever done to you. Let you down."

"You're embarrassing yourself now!" snarled Mr Big. "Go to bed!" Mum bowed her head and tottered out of the study. "It's none of your business how I speak to her. She's my property now," he continued to Dad and Frank with a sinister smile.

The boy realised this man was bad. Bad beyond redemption.

The crime boss then turned his attention to the loot piled on his desk. He picked up a wad of money. First he sniffed it. Then he kissed it. Finally he ran his fingers along the edges of the notes and put his ear next to them. A huge smile spread across his little fat face.

"Money…" he murmured to himself, as if under a spell. "Lots and lots of lovely money."

"There must be half a million, guv'nor," said Fingers.

"Not too shabby for a night's work, gentlemen. Not too shabby at all."

Like throwing a dog a bone, Mr Big threw a bundle each to his two trusty henchmen, Fingers and Thumbs.

"There's your share," said the boss.

The two men looked happy enough with their spoils.

"Thanks, guv'nor," said Fingers.

"Yeah, thanks a million, guv'nor," added Thumbs excitedly. "Now I can buy some more football stickers for my collection."

Frank and his father shared a look. Football stickers! What was he? Ten years old?

Next to Mr Big was a huge tin marked **CAVIAR**. He pushed in a little gold spoon and lifted out hundreds of the little black fish eggs.

"Ronnie? Reggie?" he called.

*Who are they?* thought Frank.

Two fat cats stood up, arched their backs and bared their fangs.

"Ronnie!"

The first cat licked the spoon and gobbled down the caviar greedily as Reggie hissed.

"Don't you worry, Reggie. Here's yours."

Mr Big then flicked a dollop of caviar into the air, which the beast caught in its mouth. The two cats **purred.**

"Chang!" ordered Big.

"Yes, master," replied the butler.

"Dump the rest of the loot in the safe for me."

"With pleasure, master," said the butler. He pulled a picture frame to one side, revealing a safe behind. Chang pressed four buttons on the keypad…

*BEEP! BOOP! BLEEP! BLOOP!*

…and the safe door whirred open.

Frank stole a look inside. The metal box was completely stacked full of gold bars and fifty-pound notes.

One by one, the butler placed the new bundles neatly in.

When Chang had finished, Frank spoke up. "Mr Big! This isn't fair! What about my dad's share?"

A deathly silence descended on the study.

"What did you say to me?" demanded Mr Big. His little piggy eyes were popping in anger.

"Nothing," replied Dad, not wanting to cause any trouble. "The boy doesn't mean anything by it."

"It wasn't nothing. What did you say to me, you nasty little **cockroach**?"

# CHAPTER

## BURSTING A BRAIN

All eyes in Mr Big's study were on Frank. This little wretch in a dirty old pair of pyjamas had dared to speak up to the crime boss.

"My dad drove the getaway car," said Frank. "You would never have got away with the robbery without him. He deserves a share of the loot!"

Mr Big started laughing.

"HA! HA! HA!"

Then Fingers started laughing.

"HA! HA! HA!"

Then Thumbs.

"HA! HA! HA!"

Finally even the unsmiling Chang made a noise that sounded a little like a laugh. "Haw haw haw!"

Ronnie and Reggie purred.

"What's so funny?" demanded the boy.

"What's so funny," began Mr Big, "is that your daddy owes ME money!"

A worried look swept across Dad's face. "But, Mr Big, that's not what we agreed. You promised tonight would clear all my debts."

Mr Big waddled over from behind his desk until he came nose to nose with Dad. The crime boss stared deep into the man's eyes, and blew a plume of smoke from his cigar into his face. This made Dad cough and splutter.

"One night!" began Big. "One night's work! Don't make me laugh. You seem to have forgotten. You borrowed a huge amount of money from me!"

"It was only five hundred pounds," pleaded Dad.

"Only five hundred pounds?"

"I needed it to buy a birthday present for my boy."

"My race set!" said the boy.

"Yes."

"But, Dad!" protested Frank. "You didn't need to buy that for me! I would have done without."

"Please be quiet, mate!" said Dad.

"But you didn't pay the money back, did you?" continued Mr Big.

"I tried – I swear I did. I tried and tried to get my old job back, banger racing, but they wouldn't let me drive again."

"You owe me, Gilbert Goodie. With interest. Five hundred pounds became a thousand pounds. One thousand pounds became ten thousand pounds. Ten thousand pounds became a hundred thousand pounds."

"That's not fair!" protested Frank. "How can five hundred pounds become a hundred thousand pounds?!"

"I'm not a bank," snapped Mr Big.

"No, you just rob them!" said Frank.

"Cocky little so-and-so, aren't you?"

"But one hundred thousand pounds?!" pleaded Dad. "I will never, ever have that sort of money!"

Mr Big smiled a sinister smile. "Then you'd better keep working for me. Until you've paid off your debt."

"That's not fair!" said Frank.

"MATE! BE QUIET!" snapped Dad. "But for how long?"

"As long as I say so."

"And what if I say no?" asked Dad.

"Fingers? Thumbs?"

At once the two henchmen sprang into action.

Fingers grabbed Frank by looping his arms under the boy's. He scooped him off the floor.

"Get off me!" screamed the boy as he struggled to get away.

"Get your filthy hands off my son!"
shouted Dad.

Thumbs kicked the man's wooden leg so hard that
it collapsed from under him.

*THWACK.*

Dad fell to the floor.

*THUD!*

"DAD!" shouted Frank.

The poor man was lying on the floor. His body was broken, but not his spirit.

"If you do anything to hurt my son, I swear, I'll…"

"You'll what?" asked Big mockingly. He trod on Dad's fingers.

CRUNCH!

"OW!" Dad screamed.

"Thumbs!" ordered Mr Big. "Do your worst with the boy!"

Frank looked on in terror as the man bent back his humongous Thumbs, ready to cause damage.

*CLICK! CLICK!*

The henchman pressed them hard into the boy's ears. Frank felt like his brain was going to burst.

"ARGH!" he screamed.

## STOP!

"PLEASE!" shouted Dad. "I'll do whatever you say! Just leave my boy alone."

Mr Big smirked before finally saying, "That's enough, gentlemen."

Fingers and Thumbs put Frank down. After a moment more enjoying his power, Big took his feet off Dad's fingers. Still writhing in pain, the man scrambled up on to his knee to hug his son, who was shaking with fear.

"I'm glad you have come round to my way of thinking, Gilbert," continued Mr Big. "I will be in touch about the next job very soon."

Frank kneeled down to help Dad reattach his wooden leg. Suddenly the boy spied one of the wads of cash lying by his feet. It must have fallen off Mr Big's desk as the suitcase was emptied. There in crisp fifty-pound notes was the answer to so many of his and his father's problems.

When he thought no one was looking, Frank moved his left foot slowly forward to cover it. If he kept his nerve, he could craftily slide it out of the room.

"My master thanks you for your visit. Now it is time to leave," announced Chang.

Frank kept his foot pressed to the floor as he and his father were shown out of the study.

After a few paces, Big barked, "STOP!"

The pair did what they were told.

"Why are you walking funny?" he demanded.

"Who? Me?" asked the boy innocently.

"Yes, you. We know why that crippled father of yours walks funny."

Unsurprisingly the two goons laughed again at their boss's cruelty. "Ha! Ha!"

"I'm not walking funny," replied Frank.

"Take a few steps, then," said Mr Big.

The boy did as he was told, dragging his left foot.

**"What is that under your foot?"**

"Nothing," lied the boy.

Mr Big bristled. The boy was testing the man's patience.

**"Thumbs!"** ordered Big.

The brute knew what to do. He marched over to Frank, wrapped his arms round his chest and lifted him off the ground.

All eyes looked down at the bundle of cash that the boy had slid halfway across the study.

"Sorry, Dad," whispered Frank.

Dad gave his son a supportive smile.

"It seems we have a thief amongst us!" announced Mr Big.

"Please, please, Mr Big, sir, have mercy on the boy," begged Dad.

The crime boss waddled over to Frank, and stared straight at him. Frank took a deep breath. What was this nasty little man going to do?

The answer was a smile. "Boy, I am impressed," began Big. "Very impressed. Stealing from Mr Big himself. That takes some guts. You should come and live here with me and your mother."

Dad looked to his son, fear blazing in his eyes.

"NEVER!" shouted Frank.

"Never say never," replied Mr Big. "Think about it."

"I've thought about it. It's never."

"I could train you up."

"Come on, Dad," said Frank, tugging on his father's sleeve. "We have to go."

Just as the pair had reached the study door, Mr Big called after the boy. "One day all this could be yours."

"I would rather die."

"That can be arranged," purred Mr Big.

# CHAPTER 39

# A FIGURE IN THE SHADOWS

Frank and his father trudged through the wind and rain in silence until they found a train station. There they huddled together for warmth on a bench on the platform, waiting for the first cold, empty train to take them back into town.

"Your mum does love you, you know," said Dad.

Frank said nothing. All that had happened during the night had brought back the feelings of hurt, and deepened them.

"She never used to drink like that," said Dad.

"It made me sad."

"Come on, I think we both need a **huggle**."

The pair held on to each other until the train trundled into the station. By the time they'd reached their block of flats, dawn was breaking. With the lift in the block still out of order, they climbed the flights and flights of steps. When Dad finally put the key in the front door, both were weary beyond words. As they entered the flat, the door to the living room opened. A figure appeared out of the shadows.

Frank gripped on to his father in fear.

"Good morning, boys!" It was only Auntie Flip.

"Oh, good morning, Auntie Flip!" said Dad.

Both he and his son had completely forgotten she was babysitting.

"Sorry you were here all night," said Dad. "I saw you asleep when I got back and thought I'd leave you to it," he added.

"Oh my word, look at the state of you!" said the lady as she frantically started rubbing the dirt off their clothes with her hand. When the mud stains wouldn't budge, Flip did Frank's most hated thing.

The lady took out her handkerchief, **spat** on it and began vigorously wiping the mud off. Then she sniffed her handkerchief. "This is cow dung!" she exclaimed. "Where on earth have you been?"

"We just popped out to get a pint of milk," lied Dad.

"Straight from the cow?" she asked.

"Er, no. It came from Raj's shop," added the boy, hoping to make the lie sound a little more believable. "I think we must have stepped in a cowpat on the way back."

"Is that so? Well, I could murder a cup of tea," said Auntie Flip. "Where is that milk?"

"What milk?" asked Dad.

"The milk you bought."

"We took it back to the shop," said Frank.

"Why?" asked the lady.

"It was off," replied Dad.

"We should have guessed!" continued Frank. "It was on special offer. But I'm sure Raj could sell it as cheese."

Flip looked at them both quizzically. The lady knew something was up, but what exactly? She stuffed her handkerchief back up her sleeve and glanced at her watch.

"Oh dear. Is that the time? We'd better get going."

"Where?" asked Dad.

"Don't tell me you've both forgotten!"

Dad and Frank looked at each other. After the drama of the night they had indeed forgotten. But what exactly had they forgotten?

"Sorry, yes, we have actually forgotten," said Frank.

"Church, of course!" exclaimed Flip.

"Oh yes. Church!" said Dad, trying to sound a little bit excited and failing miserably.

"Happy Father's Day, Dad."

"Thank you, mate."

Auntie Flip looked on with a proud smile. "*Beautiful!* And don't fret – I have written a special *Father's Day poem* for you to read to the entire congregation."

Father and son shared a pained look.

# CHAPTER

## 40

# EMPTY CHAIRS

"Welcome, welcome and thrice welcome!" said Reverend Judith as Frank, Dad and Auntie Flip entered the church, soaked from the thunderstorm still raging outside. "I hope I will be able to find you three seats together. Do you want to sit together?"

"If we possibly can," said Auntie Flip.

Frank looked around the church. It was bursting with… chairs. Empty chairs. Sadly, the ever-eager Reverend Judith had not been able to conjure up many worshippers, even though it was Father's Day. There was just one old dear sitting halfway back, her faulty hearing aid letting off a high-pitched whistle.

EEEEEEEEEEEEEEEEEE!!!

"This way, please," said Reverend Judith as she guided the trio to the front of the church.

As they passed the old dear, she shouted out, "When's the tea and biscuits, Vicar? I was promised tea and biscuits."

"Tea and biscuits will be served straight after the service," replied the vicar with a smile.

"I'll come back in an hour, then," said the old dear, and she got up and walked out of the church.

Poor Reverend Judith tried to hide her disappointment, and carried on guiding her congregation of three to their seats. "These three here all right for you?"

"Perfect, thank you," replied Flip. "And may I say you are looking *lovely* today."

"Why, thank you," said the vicar, taken aback.

"Have you done something to your hair?"

"I just ran a comb through it," shrugged the vicar.

"Well, it looks *delightful*."

"How *delightful* of you to say so."

Auntie Flip and the vicar shared bashful grins. Frank had never witnessed his babysitter behave like this before.

"Dad!" the boy whispered into his father's ear.

"Yes?"

"What's going on between those two?"

"I don't know."

Neither had ever given much thought to Auntie Flip's love life before.

"Shush!" shushed Auntie Flip. "Please be mindful of the rest of the congregation."

"There's nobody here!" protested the boy.

"This is a church! They are here in spirit," replied Auntie Flip. "Carry on, Vicar!"

"Thank you, Flip!" As soon as she began her welcome speech, rain poured from the roof on to her, as if someone had turned on a tap. Judith tried to avoid it by moving, but every time she did she managed to find an even worse spot. The vicar hadn't been lying all these years: the roof was in dire need of repair.

"Welcome, one and all, to this special Father's Day service. It is super to see so many new faces here today."

Frank looked around to see if anyone else had come in. They hadn't. By "so many" she must have meant "two".

"Now, to begin today I want to ask one particular father and son to join me at the altar to read their special *Father's Day poem* to the rest of the congregation."

With **heavy** hearts, father and son went up to the altar, and turned round to face the sea of empty chairs.

"'Father's Day', by Auntie Flip," began the boy.

*"I love you, Daddy, I really do."*

Rain poured from the roof on to the boy's head as Dad took over for his part.

*"And I love you, son, I really do.*
*The day you were born I was so happy,*
*Even though I had to change your nappy."*

Dad had been looking smug that he'd not been getting soaked. However, suddenly the rain came through the roof with such force it was as if a bucket of water was being emptied over his head.

*"I always made sure I deposited a gift for you,*
*A number one or a number two."*

Just then the doors at the back of the church swung open.

# CREAK!

In marched Sergeant Scoff, who took a seat at the front.

Father and son looked at each other nervously. What was he doing here? They tried to carry on as if nothing was wrong. If they'd thought the poem couldn't get any worse, they were mistaken.

*"Looking at you would always make me dotty,*
*Your eyes, your toes, even your little botty,"*
continued Dad.

The doors swung open again.

# CREAK!

This time, in marched police officer after police officer after police officer. They took their helmets off because they were in a church, then instantly put them on again to avoid the water leaking from the roof.

Frank glanced across to Reverend Judith, who was **beaming** to see her church filling up. With some hesitation the boy continued with the poem.

*"Darling Daddy, you are the best…"*

But before he could read the next line Sergeant Scoff jumped in with glee.

*"No, he's not – he's under arrest!"*

# CHAPTER 41

# GUILTY

The police had found the getaway car in the field. The rain had washed most of the yellow paint off the Mini to reveal the Union Jack underneath. There was no doubt that the car was **Queenie**. This led the police to their prime suspect, the car's owner, Gilbert Goodie. The man was arrested in church, charged at the police station and then locked up in prison. Weeks passed, until the day of the trial arrived. It came as no surprise that Dad was found…

"GUILTY!" The head of the jury announced their verdict.

All eyes in the courtroom then turned to Judge Pillar. The unsmiling old man was seated front and centre on what looked like a throne. He was draped in red robes with a strange old-fashioned wig plonked on his head. As he was the one on trial, Dad was standing in the dock. A smug-looking Sergeant Scoff was at his side, guarding him. Downstairs in the courtroom sat the jury, lawyers, court clerks and police officers. Upstairs in the gallery sat various onlookers, including Frank and Auntie Flip. A few rows behind them sat Fingers and Thumbs. Frank guessed Mr Big must have sent them to report back on everything.

"Mr Goodie, the jury has found you guilty as charged. May I add that I am extremely disappointed in you," continued Judge Pillar. "You have a young son, yet you involve yourself in the world of organised crime. Robbing a bank no less! Stealing half a million pounds! Money, I might add, that has never been recovered. You must know where the money is hidden, and yet, Mr Goodie, you refuse to inform the police. You must have had accomplices, but you will not name them. This no doubt is the criminals' code of honour."

Frank looked over his shoulder at Fingers and Thumbs, who smiled at the boy menacingly.

"For any decent, law-abiding citizen, there is no honour in this. None at all. You are a bad man, Mr Goodie. And, worst of all, a bad dad. A very bad dad."

That hit Gilbert like a ton of bricks. He looked over to his son with tears in his eyes, as the judge announced the sentence. "Gilbert Goodie, I sentence you to ten years in prison!"

# NO ONE SAYS NO

"DAD!" shouted Frank as his father was led away in handcuffs by Sergeant Scoff. "NO!" The boy was sobbing. He would be a grown-up by the time his dad was let out of prison.

"I'm so sorry, mate!" called Dad. "Please take care of him, Auntie Flip!"

"I will!" called the lady as she took out her lace handkerchief from up her sleeve to dab the boy's eyes. "Don't cry, Frank. I will look after you."

"I just want my dad," sniffed the boy.

"I know. I know. I'm sorry I'm not your dad. But we'll just have to make the best of it all somehow. Now come along."

Auntie Flip took Frank's hand and led him out of the courtroom, but their path was blocked by Fingers and Thumbs.

"Excuse us!" said the lady, but the pair wouldn't budge.

"It's a good job your daddy didn't squeal," said Fingers. "Who knows what might have happened to you? Or to him, in prison."

"Me six brothers are all in the nick," announced Thumbs.

"You must be so proud," said Auntie Flip. "Now, please get out of the way."

Still the pair blocked their path.

"Who are you?" demanded Flip.

"We are friends of the boy's father," replied Fingers.

"They are not friends!" said Frank. "They are the ones who got him in this awful mess."

Fingers put one of his long, thin fingers to his lips. "Be careful what you say."

"Just let us go!" said the boy, trying and failing to push past the two henchmen.

"Don't be in such a rush, boy. We come bearing an invitation," said Fingers. "Mr Big has a proposition for you. He would like you to come over to the house."

"I said never!" said the boy.

"LET US PASS!" demanded Auntie Flip. "Or I will use force!" She raised her handbag, ready to whack the two men if need be.

"No one, but no one, says no to Mr Big," said Fingers. He stepped aside, and did a little mock bow to the pair as they passed. Just as they reached the door, the henchman called after them. "No one *alive*, that is!"

# CHAPTER

## 43

# PONGY CHEESE

That night at Auntie Flip's house, Frank soaked his pillow with tears. Flip heard him from the kitchen downstairs, and brought him up a new pillow. She sat on the side of the little pink bed in her little pink spare room, and stroked the boy's hair.

"Right now, young Frank, it's as if you are walking through a storm," said Auntie Flip, "but I promise you in time the rain will lift a little."

It didn't. Day after day Frank felt as if he was walking through **thunder** and *lightning.*

The boy was bullied at school for having a father who was "banged up". If anything went missing at school, he always got the blame. One particularly unpleasant girl in his class said, "Frank's old man is a thief. It stands to reason he's a dirty little thief and all."

But Frank knew in his heart that his father wasn't a thief. He was a good man who had done a bad thing. Dad had got himself into a mountain of debt trying to do the best he could for his son. Now Frank had to do the best for his father. But how?

Auntie Flip's little house was overflowing with antique bits and pieces. There was barely enough room for Frank, as every chair or table or cupboard was piled up with thimbles, porcelain dolls, leather-bound books, animal figurines and old-fashioned teddy bears.

Life with Auntie Flip couldn't be more different from how life had been with his father. The lady would sit over him as he did his homework, making sure he dotted every "i" and crossed every "t". Sometimes she would even correct the teacher's spelling mistakes.

"I am sorry to say your History teacher is an ignoramus! She can't even spell 'Bayeux'!"

They never, ever had chips for tea. Instead the lady would cook him one of her quiches, which the boy always found disgusting. Auntie Flip was **Queen of the Quiche.** The savoury pastry was about the only thing she ate.

Her quiche recipes were not to most people's tastes:

**Pickled Onion and Beetroot**
**Curried Egg and Cabbage**
**Pongy Cheese and Turnip**
**Partridge, Parsnip and Pear**
**Spam, Spam, Spam and More Spam**
**Eel and Artichoke**
**Prawn and Seagull's Egg**
**Brussels Sprouts and Goat's Curd**

After-dinner entertainment was always "poetry hour", though this hour would often stretch to two or three.

"This next one is called *'Ode to a Tree'* by me," she would announce grandly, before reading it out loud.

*"O tree, O tree,*
*O lovely, lovely tree,*
*As you dance in the breeze*
*With perfect ease,*
*I think if only I could be*
*So wondrously free,*
*But it's plain to see*
*I will never be a tree."*

# "Zzzz! Zzzz! Zzzz! Zzzz!"

The boy would pretend to be asleep. It was the only way to make her stop.

As the days turned into weeks, and weeks into months,

the unlikely pair became close. Frank grew to love the lady. She had shown him kindness when he'd needed it most. When his father was sent to prison, Frank thought his mother might call him. But she never did. Auntie Flip was all he had.

Soon she and Frank had settled into a cosy routine. **Friday** evenings the pair would visit the local library where Flip worked, and the boy would forget his troubles for a while as he lost himself in the pages of books.

He even learned to love poetry. **Saturday** mornings they would take a walk in the park. Flip would give the boy a coin to make a wish, but the wish never came true. His father stayed locked up in prison.

**Sunday** mornings Flip would take Frank to

church, which was just as well as they would be the only people there. Each night Flip would shake out her lace tablecloth and set her little wooden dining table for two. When, one night, a third place setting was laid, the boy was naturally intrigued.

# CHAPTER

# 44

# SNEEZE JUICE

"Super to see you again, young Frank!" said the lady as the boy opened the front door for her. She was carrying a bouquet of wild flowers.

"Hello, Vicar," said the boy. They stood there looking at each other for a moment.

"Can I come in?" she asked.

"If that is the vicar, please let her in at once!" called Flip from the kitchen.

"That makes a nice change," said Reverend Judith.

Flip wafted towards them wearing her floatiest, floweriest dress. She became quite emotional upon seeing the flowers.

"For me?" she asked.

"Yes!" said Judith. "I picked them myself."

"No one has ever brought me flowers before. Thank you so, so much." Flip sniffed the flowers and then instantly sneezed on them.

# "ATCHOO!"

"Are you all right?" asked the vicar.

"Yes, yes. I am very slightly allergic to flowers but I love them." Flip arranged them in a vase on the dining table. "**ATCHOOOO!**" she sneezed again, louder this time.

 "So you've never been married?" asked the vicar.

"Married?" scoffed Flip. "I've never been kissed!"

"Really?" said the vicar.

"Yes. Not once. All that romance nonsense passed me by years ago."

It was such a sad thought, to have lived a whole life without love, that neither Frank nor Judith knew what to say.

Fortunately Flip broke the silence. "Let's all sit down for dinner," she announced.

The three took their places at the table.

"I hope you like rabbit and dandelion quiche!" said Flip.

The boy grimaced.

The vicar replied, "I have never tried it, but I'm sure it will be delicious. Let me say grace."

Flip closed her eyes in prayer, so the boy did the same.

"Dear Lord, may you bless this quiche this night. And bless the special parishioner who cooked it. Amen."

"Amen."

"Amen," copied Frank, though he didn't know what "amen" meant.

The vicar took a bite of her food and grimaced.

"How is the quiche?" asked Flip.

"Delicious!" lied the lady. Somehow Flip's quiches were always rubbery and hard to bite into.

"Wonderful. So how was church on Sunday, Reverend?"

"Judith is fine."

The pair giggled. The boy felt like a gooseberry, sitting between them.

"How was church on Sunday, Judith? ATCHOO!" The sneeze was much louder this time. "Apologies, Judith. I think some of my sneeze juice sprayed over you."

"No matter," said Judith, wiping snot from her eye.

"Frank and I are so sorry we missed Sunday service. Tell Judith where we were, Frankie."

"At a poetry society competition," sighed the boy, still bored at the memory of the weekend.

"Oh, how did you do?" asked the vicar.

"Very well," replied Auntie Flip. "I came ninety-seventh!"

"Congratulations. Ninety-seventh!"

"Thank you." Flip blushed with pride.

"How many entrants were there?"

"Ninety-eight," replied Frank.

"Well, that's not bad," said Judith, trying to look on the bright side.

"One poetess got disqualified for biting another competitor," added Flip. "She said she'd stolen a rhyme. She rhymed **gherkin** with **twerkin'**."

"Oh dear," said Judith, who suddenly seemed put off her quiche.

"That was the only good bit," said Frank with a smirk.

"No, it wasn't!" snapped Flip. "As you can imagine, the poetry society has a zero-tolerance policy for biting."

"I can imagine."

# ❀ "ATCHOO!"

Another noseful of snot **flew** across the dining table, drenching the vicar.

"Shall we move the flowers?" asked Judith.

"Yes, that's probably a good idea. Frank? Be a good boy."

The boy picked up the vase, and took it into the kitchen.

"So how many worshippers did you have at church on Sunday?" asked Flip.

The vicar looked hesitant to answer. "Just one," she murmured.

"That's not too bad, Judith. At least one person came."

"No. It was just me," replied the vicar.

"Oh dear."

"Oh dear indeed."

Frank came back into the dining room, and announced, "You know, Dad and I will come to church every Sunday…"

The two grown-ups looked at each other, concerned. What was the boy talking about? His father was looking at a ten-year stretch. He wasn't going to Sunday service any time soon.

"...if you help me break him out of prison."

# CHAPTER 45

# MASTERPLAN

"**I am a vicar!**" exclaimed the vicar.

"**And I am a librarian!**" exclaimed the librarian. "We can't be – I think the phrase is – 'busting' your father out of prison."

"**PLEASE LISTEN TO ME FIRST!**" said the boy. The words tumbled out as Frank told the two old ladies the whole story. How Dad had borrowed money from the evil Mr Big, and how the debt had spiralled. How his father had been tricked into taking part in the robbery. How Dad had kept quiet in the trial to save his son from being hurt by Big's henchmen, Fingers and Thumbs. The boy finished up by saying, "That judge was wrong. My dad is not a bad dad. He is a good man who did a bad thing.

He did it to save me from getting hurt. Dad doesn't deserve to be in prison. We need to help him escape."

The two ladies looked at each other in silence. It was Reverend Judith who spoke first. "A great wrong has been done to your father, no doubt about it. I wish we could do something to right that wrong."

"But with respect, Judith, two wrongs don't make a right!" said Flip. The lady then turned to Frank. "I'm sorry, but you're asking us to take part in something very wrong. I promise you, those ten years will pass before you know it."

This made the boy mightily angry. **"Ten years! TEN YEARS?** I will be twenty-one in ten years. An old man!"

Frank stood up, knocking his chair over. *BANG!*

"And you know what, Auntie Flip? I *hate* quiche! And poetry! I want my dad back! And if you won't help me I'll do it all by myself!"

Frank ran out of the dining room and up the stairs to his bedroom.

"FRANKIE!" called Flip after him.

The boy slammed the door and lay down on his little pink bed, his legs dangling off the end. He could hear that the two ladies were talking downstairs. Frank picked up an empty glass on the bedside table. He slid off the bed, and put his ear to the glass and the glass on the floor so he could listen to what they were saying.

"Those two henchmen have been terrorising people all over town," said Judith. "They need to be stopped. They even stole the gold communion goblet from the church."

"Dreadful! I came face to face with them in court. A truly nasty pair."

"It's not fair that the boy's father is paying the price for their misdeeds."

"You forget he drove the getaway car. There's no escaping that. Gilbert committed a serious crime."

"But he only did it to protect his son!"

"Oh, it's such a mess. But if my nephew did try to escape from prison he would be captured and sent straight back. And get a longer sentence!"

"We have to do something, though."

"If only there was some way of putting all that money back."

# *PING!*

The boy's brain lit up with an idea. That was exactly what he could do to help his father: put the money back in the bank. How could Dad be guilty if no money was missing?

Trembling with excitement, Frank wonkily wrote down his masterplan.

# MASTERPLAN

1.  Break into Mr Big's country house.

2.  Steal half a million pounds out of Mr Big's safe.

3.  Break into the bank.

4.  Put half a million pounds in the bank's vault.

It was simple but brilliant. There was just one problem. The boy had absolutely no idea how he could put any of this plan into action. All Frank knew was that it would be impossible to do it alone. He needed a grown-up to help him. But who?

# CHAPTER

## 46

# A RIDDLE

There was one person Frank knew who could give
him some advice. His friendly local newsagent.

## DING!

"Ah, my favourite customer!" exclaimed Raj on
seeing the boy. The newsagent tried to be his usual
jolly self, but there was sadness in his eyes. The man
was sweeping up shards of broken glass from the
floor. Someone had smashed in the front window of
his shop.

"Are you all right, Raj? What happened?"

Raj picked up a brick from the counter. "This came
through the window in the middle of the night. It
came with a note attached to it. Look."

It read:

**WE DEMAND £200 A WEEK OR NEXT TIME THE BRICK WILL HIT YOU.**

"Fingers and Thumbs?" asked Frank.

"Of course."

"They need to be stopped."

"I know, I know. I don't know where I'm going to find the money."

"I'm sorry I don't have any today."

"That's all right, young sir. I know times are hard with your father in prison." Raj put a comforting arm round the boy. "Please help yourself to anything in my shop for free."

"Free?" Frank couldn't believe his ears.

"Yes, anything you like."

"Wow! Thank you, Raj."

"Up to a value of **eight p.**"

"Oh." The boy couldn't hide his disappointment. He picked up the smallest chocolate bar he could see.

"That's **ten p**, young man."

"Oh."

"Pass it to me, please," said Raj, gesturing with his hands. The boy did what he was told. Raj then unwrapped the bar, took a bite off the end and passed it back to the boy.

"That was a **two-p** bite. There you go. We are even now."

"Thanks, Raj." Frank was too hungry to worry about Raj's **gob gloop** on the bar, and happily demolished it in seconds. "My dad isn't the real bad guy, you know."

"I'm sure. He is a good man, your father."

"Fingers and Thumbs made him do it!"

"That makes sense. And they are free to threaten

everyone in town while your poor father sits in jail."

"I can't bear it."

"I can imagine. Have a free penny chew."

"Thanks, Raj," replied Frank, popping a raspberry fizz in his pocket for later. "Dad got caught up in this really bad debt that spiralled way out of control. He was only trying to help me. Now I need to help him. I just need to steal the **half a million pounds** from the men who stole it in the first place, and put it back in the bank."

Raj pondered on this. "I suppose if nothing was stolen, then the judge might let your father out of prison."

"That's what I'm hoping!"

"But how on earth are you going to steal the money and put it back in the bank?"

The boy looked down to the floor. "I have absolutely no idea."

"Oh," replied the newsagent. "I am sorry I have no idea, either."

"The only person I know who could help me do all that is my dad," said Frank.

"Well, you could always wait ten years until he was let out of prison and do it then."

Frank looked at the newsagent. Surely no one was that daft. "There would be no point, Raj, as he would have served his time by then."

"Oh yes. Silly me!" The newsagent slapped himself in the face.

"To get my dad out of prison I have to get him out of prison."

Raj looked puzzled. "That is like a riddle, but, yes, you are right. The problem is your dad was sent to the most high-security jail in the country. In a hundred years no one has ever escaped from **Wrongfoot Prison**."

## "No?"

"Wrongfoot is where they put all the naughtiest criminals."

"It's not fair!" exclaimed the boy. "My dad doesn't

deserve to be in there. I hate not being with him. Now I have to live with his aunt, Auntie Flip."

Raj suddenly remembered something. "I had Auntie Flip in here this morning. She wanted to know if I sold goose."

"Goose?"

"She said she needed one for a quiche."

"Oh no! That will be for my dinner."

"I told her she might be able to catch one down by the ponds. She'd never been into my shop before."

"Then how did you know it was her?" asked the boy.

"She looks exactly like your father. Older, of course, and a lady, but I could immediately see the resemblance. The same sticky-out ears that you have. No offence!"

"None taken!" lied the boy.

"I asked her if she and your father were related, and she explained who she was. To my eyes, they could be twins!"

# Gilbert and Auntie Flip

Frank screwed up his face. "You think so?"

"Put some glasses on him and he would be her double!"

"Ha! Ha!" the boy chuckled. His eyes widened as he started to see his plan unfold in his mind. "Raj, you are a genius!"

"Am I?"

"YES!" The boy was so happy he wanted to dance. He grabbed hold of Raj and gave him a big kiss on his balding head. "Thank you, thank you, thank you!"

"What did I do?" The newsagent was befuddled.

"I am sorry, Raj. It's a secret for now!"

*DING!*

The boy skipped off down the street. All he had to do now was persuade Auntie Flip to swap places with his dad in prison. How hard could that be?

# CHAPTER 47

# WHERE DID YOU GET THAT GOOSE?

"NO!" shouted Auntie Flip. "NO! NO! NO! NO! NO! Absolutely one hundred per cent no."

"So that's a no?" asked Frank.

"YES! That's a NO! Now finish up your goose and gooseberry quiche."

The pair were sitting together at the dining table in Auntie Flip's little house. The boy had had the tiniest inkling that his great-aunt wouldn't like the idea of swapping places with his dad in prison, but he wasn't giving up yet.

Frank took a bite of his quiche. As usual, it tasted horrible. "Auntie Flip?"

"Yes?"

"Where did you get the goose?"

The lady looked sheepish. "From a shop."

"What shop?"

"The goose shop," she said, avoiding his gaze. Flustered, she got up from the table and disappeared into the kitchen. It was the perfect opportunity for Frank to hurl the rest of the quiche out of the window.

# WHIZZ!
# SPLAT!

Unfortunately Frank hadn't realised the window was shut, and the quiche trickled down the glass.

"Oops," said the boy as he ran to the window and tried to clean the bits of goose, gooseberry and pastry off the window with his sleeve. Then he took the empty plate into the kitchen.

"That was absolutely delicious, Auntie Flip," lied Frank.

The lady softened. No one had ever complimented

her on her quiches before. "Oh, thank you. Would you like some more?"

"No, no, no," replied the boy, a little too quickly. "I am completely full. You cooked such a delicious meal. That was one of your top fifty quiches of all time. Now, come on, let me do the washing-up tonight."

"What a good boy you are. Thank you. I will dry."

Frank stood at the sink, and began washing the plates. He realised if he was going to reel his great-aunt into his plan, he was going to have to do it very gently. "The vicar is such a smart lady, isn't she?"

"Oh yes, very much so."

Passing a freshly washed dinner plate to his great-aunt, the boy said, "You should invite her over for dinner again."

"We'll see," replied Flip.

"What is stopping you?"

"I don't know. Fear."

"Of what?"

"Of what might happen. Between me and her. I like her, you see, Frankie. I like her very much."

"Well, surely that is nothing to be scared of."

The lady let out a sad sigh. "My whole life has been ruled by fear. Maybe that is why I've never been kissed."

"Maybe. Now seems like the perfect time to change."

The boy let this settle in to Auntie Flip's mind.

"So how long exactly would I have to swap places with your father for?" she asked tentatively.

"Just one night," the boy replied casually. "Just one night in prison. Think of it as a little holiday. Then, with Dad on the outside, he and I can steal the money back off Mr Big and put it in the bank. Then the next morning you can swap again."

"First thing in the morning?"

"Yes. First thing."

"I hear the breakfasts in prison aren't great."

"You won't have to eat the breakfast."

"I'm not sure."

"Think of it as an adventure."

"I've never had an adventure."

"Well, now is the time to start. And I wouldn't be surprised if Judith saw you as a hero!"

"You think so?"

"I know so."

Flip took a deep breath. "Frankie, the most excitement I've ever had in my life is when I got to charge someone a twenty-three-pound fine for a library book that had been overdue for a year," she confessed. "This is all too…"

"Thrilling?" asked the boy.

"Yes, that's it! Thrilling!" The lady's face lit up. "Not too thrilling, just thrilling! Frank, this is madness, but I'm in!"

"YES!"

CHAPTER

# WRONGFOOT

Visiting day at the prison was every Saturday. For Frank it couldn't come soon enough. **Wrongfoot Prison** was a big, ugly building with a big, ugly wall around it. Visiting hours were strict, and Frank and Flip joined the long queue that snaked around the wall.

There were pregnant women in leggings, screaming toddlers, weepy mothers, terrifying shaven-headed men and even more terrifying shaven-headed women.

Flip was holding a freshly baked quiche in a tin that was a gift for Frank's father, pigeon and plum.

The trouble was she was so frazzled with nerves she was rattling it like crazy. It was as if she had a hundred jumping frogs in that tin.

*RATTLE!*
    *RATTLE!*
*RATTLE!*

"Try to keep that thing still, Auntie Flip!" hissed Frank. "Everyone is staring."

The lady looked around to see that there were hundreds of sets of eyes staring back at her. Even the screaming toddlers had momentarily stopped screaming and were **gawping**.

"There's nothing to see here!" announced Auntie Flip, which made her seem guilty or nutty or, even worse, both. "Just a quiche in a tin. Pay me no heed!"

Frank snatched the tin from her.

"Just stay calm," the boy reassured her. "This is going to be a **doddle**."

"A **doddle**! I haven't slept a wink all week!"

Flip had spent all morning trimming and styling her hair so it looked as much like her nephew's as possible. The lady had put on her **longest,** floatiest dress too, in the hope that the man would be able to fit into it.

The plan was that at just the right moment Frank would drop the quiche on the floor, and then Flip and Dad would scramble under the table to pick up the pieces. While under the table they would swap clothes. If all went to plan, then Dad would leave prison disguised as Auntie Flip, and Auntie Flip would stay in prison disguised as Dad. What could possibly go wrong?

"What's in that tin?" barked the prison guard as the pair entered the visitors' room. His name badge read **Mr Swivel**. It was hard not to notice him, with his bulging glass eye, which swivelled in his head as he spoke.

"It's a q-q-q..." Auntie Flip was so nervous she couldn't answer.

The guard looked at the lady. "What's a q-q-q?"

"A quiche, Mr Swivel, sir!" said Frank, opening the tin to prove it. People would often try to smuggle things into prison – booze, mobile telephones, weapons and all sorts – so everything had to be checked. Mr Swivel put his nose inside the tin and sniffed the quiche. His face turned a shade of **green**.

"What on earth is in that thing?" he demanded.

"Pigeon and plum," answered Flip proudly.

"Eurgh!" replied Mr Swivel. "Move along! Chop-chop!"

The pair shuffled into the visitors' room. Everything in there was grey: grey walls, grey furniture, grey people. Dad was sitting on the far side of the room in his grey prison overalls. As soon as he saw his son, he jumped up out of his chair with tears in his eyes. The man looked happy and sad all at once.

"MATE!" he cried.

"DAD!" exclaimed Frank as he rushed towards the man with his arms wide open.

They came together in the tightest hug, which neither ever wanted to break.

"I'm so happy to see you, mate," sniffed Dad.

"And I'm even happier to see you. I've missed you so much." Then, "Dad?" the boy whispered.

"Yeah?"

"This is all going to seem very strange, but you have to trust me. I'm going to get you out of here."

"OUT?"

"Not too loud, Dad," whispered the boy.

"Sorry."

"You need to trust me and do exactly what I tell you."

Auntie Flip had now caught up with the pair, and was standing behind Frank. "Good afternoon. I have made you a quiche!" she announced, rather stiffly.

"Oh, thank you, Auntie Flip," replied Dad with a pained look on his face. The man had grown up eating his aunt's awful quiches, and was lucky to still be alive.

"Let's all sit down and talk, shall we?" said the boy as the prison guard circled, keeping an eye on everyone.

As Mr Swivel passed out of earshot, Frank whispered, "In a moment, I'm going to drop the quiche on the floor. It's going to break. You and Auntie Flip are going to disappear under the table to pick up the pieces. But really you are going to change clothes…"

"You *what*?" replied Dad.

"Trust me, Dad. Then tonight me and you are going to put the money that was stolen back in the bank and get you out of here for good."

"Mate!" Dad's eyes lit up. "You are a **genius**. You take after your father!"

"If you were a **genius**, you wouldn't be in here," said Auntie Flip unhelpfully.

The man shot his aunt a look.

"Let's not fall out before we've even started!" said the boy. He held the quiche in his hands. "Now I'm going to drop this in three, two, one…"

# BOING!

It didn't break.

The quiche **bounced**.

Frank caught it on the way back up.

"What on earth do you put in these things?" said Dad.

"I don't like to divulge my secret recipes," replied his aunt.

"Have another go!" said Dad.

The boy threw the quiche down on the floor again as hard as he could…

# BOING!

...but it bounced right back up and hit the ceiling.

# *SPLAT!*

It stuck there.

"Oh no," said Frank.

The three stared up at it.

"What are we going to do now?" asked Dad.

"Let me climb on your shoulders," replied the boy.

His father quickly hoisted the boy up.

"What are you doing?" demanded Mr Swivel.

"Oh! The quiche slipped out of my hand!" lied Flip.

"And it stuck on the *ceiling*?" said the prison guard.

"Well, it is pigeon-flavoured, so maybe it flew up," she said.

Frank peeled the quiche off the ceiling. "We have it now, thank you, sir!"

"Sit down, the three of you!" ordered Mr Swivel.

They did what the prison guard said. As soon as his back was turned, Frank snapped into action.

"One last go!" said the boy.

"Fingers crossed," said Dad.

The boy slammed the quiche down as hard as he could on the floor.

# BOOF!

It broke into a hundred pieces.

"Whoops! I dropped the quiche!" announced the boy to everyone in the visitors' room.

The two grown-ups slid under the table.

**The game was on!**

# THWACK!

Just as the fearsome prison guard Mr Swivel was becoming more and more suspicious as to why these two had been under the table for so long, Flip slid up on to Dad's chair. Without her glasses and wearing Dad's prison overalls, she passed rather well for her nephew.

Next, Dad slid up on to Flip's chair. The boy had to stifle a giggle at the sight of his dad wearing one of Flip's famous *floaty* dresses. The glasses softened his face, and from a distance he might just pass as the elderly librarian.

"Stop giggling, mate!"

hissed Dad. "You'll give the game away."

"Sorry, Dad."

"I think I look rather cool," said Dad. "Though now I can't see a thing. My word, these glasses are thick!"

"I can't see now, either!" added Flip.

Dad looked down at his feet. "Oh no!"

"What, Dad?"

"There's something you forgot. My wooden leg!"

The boy looked under the table. Dad's wooden foot and ankle were poking out from the bottom of the dress.

"What's all this whispering?" demanded Mr Swivel as he twirled his stick.

"Nothing, Mr Swivel," said Dad in a voice that was a little too high.

"Nothing, Mr Swivel," said

Flip in a voice that was a little too low.

The boy glanced down to his father's wooden foot.

The guard clocked this, and his one real eye was drawn down there too. "Lady, I don't remember you having a wooden leg when you came in!" he barked.

Suddenly all eyes in the visitors' room were on this one group in the corner.

"Oh yes, Mr Swivel!" replied Dad, his voice cracking a little as he tried to sound ladylike. "Solid oak!"

"But you've got a wooden leg too," snarled the guard, his eye swivelling on to Flip.

"Yes, they run in the family!" she replied.

Frank rolled his eyes. "Well, Auntie Flip, we'd better get going," said the boy, eager to get out of there before any more suspicion was raised.

"Right you are," said the lady, getting up from her chair.

"I mean this Auntie Flip here!" said Frank, grabbing his father by the arm.

"Oh yes, of course!" said the lady. "I'd better be getting back to my prison cell, wherever that is!"

"STOP RIGHT THERE!" barked Mr Swivel. "Let's just check you really are who you say you are. Stand still! Let's see if you really do have a wooden leg. If you do, then this won't hurt at all!"

Auntie Flip stood still as Frank and his father looked on anxiously. Mr Swivel swivelled his baton, before whacking the lady hard on the leg with it.

*THWACK!*

To her credit, Flip did not cry out in pain. Instead she pursed her lips and heroically held it in. It was enough to convince Mr Swivel.

"Off you go, then!" he barked.

Auntie Flip limped off in pain, which of course only helped the illusion that her leg was wooden. Without her glasses, she walked straight into a guard.

"Oh, silly me!" she said.

Frank grabbed his father by the arm and hurried him out of the visitors' room. Just as they reached the door, their path was blocked by a wall of a man.

"OOF! Sorry!" said the boy, bumping into him. Looking up, he realised it was someone he knew only too well.

Thumbs.

# CHAPTER 50

## SEVEN BROTHERS

Thumbs had two fearsome-looking boys with him. They were the size of children but had the cold, hard faces of grown-ups.

"It's you," growled Thumbs.

"Yes, it is me," replied Frank. "Well, I would love to stop for a natter, but we must be going. Come along, Auntie Flip." He tugged at the sleeve of his father's long, *flowery* dress.

"Grrr!" The two boys growled at Frank and this unusual-looking woman, and blocked their path.

Sweat steamed up Dad's glasses. He was clearly nervous. Would Thumbs recognise him?

"If you'll excuse us, please," said Frank.

"Will? Bear?" said Thumbs.

"Yeah, Uncle Thumbs?" they replied in unison.

"This is the boy I was telling you about. The one whose racing track you've got."

Frank's face dropped. This horrible pair had his **favourite** toy in the world.

"Oh well, it's nice to know it went to a good home," lied Frank. "Nah, we smashed it up," said Will with a smirk.

"Then we ate it," added Bear.

"I hope it doesn't make you ill," replied Frank in a tone that suggested that was exactly what he wanted.

Then Thumbs turned his attention to this unusual lady trying to hide behind Frank. "Who are you?" he barked.

"Oh, this is my dad's aunt!" leaped in Frank. "Auntie Flip. You met her in court at my dad's trial, remember?"

The man-mountain peered down at the "lady". "You look different."

"That was a few weeks ago. I am very slightly older," chirped Dad, putting on his best Auntie Flip voice.

"We must have all you boys over for a play date

soon!" said Frank. "And, Thumbs? Thank you so much for not sticking your Thumbs in my ears this time. Now, come along, Auntie Flip. We have to go

right now."

The pair edged round the gang.

"Something's not right with that woman," growled Thumbs.

"She's nearly as ugly as our mum," said Will.

"No one's that ugly," added Bear.

Frank and his father didn't look back. They hurried down the corridor as fast as they could, Dad's wooden leg slowing him down.

"You didn't have a limp last time," called Thumbs.

"Run!" hissed Frank.

As soon as they'd turned a corner he asked, "Dad, d'you think Thumbs knew it was really you?"

"I dunno. He's thick as two short planks of wood, but his six brothers are all banged up in here, so he's got eyes and ears all over the prison. Auntie Flip better watch out."

Thumbs's brothers were:

**Spider.** A tattoo of a spider's web covered his face. Somehow it must have seemed like a good idea at the time.

**Gorilla.** Gorilla never bathed, and smelled like an ape. His pong was enough to knock a grown man out from a distance of one hundred metres.

**Brillo.** So called because every inch of his skin was covered in thick, black, wiry hair, with which he would scratch his victims to death like a giant Brillo Pad. Brillo was father to Will and Bear.

**Shelf.** This brother had a giant bottom that stuck out like a shelf. It was so big and **heavy** he could crush his enemies to death just by sitting on them.

**Knuckles.** He wore huge gold rings on every finger, which made his punches all the harder.

**Warts.** His face was covered in hundreds and hundreds of warts. Warts was the good-looking one in the family.

Soon Frank and his father passed through the huge prison gates.

"We made it!" said Dad.

"Just," replied Frank. "But there's no time to lose."

Escaping from prison was the easy part. Now they had an epic task ahead of them.

# CHAPTER 51

# A GRAVEYARD FOR CARS

Frank and Dad found empty seats at the back of the bus. As soon as the boy was sure no one could hear, he began telling his father all about his plan. To steal the half a million pounds from Mr Big and put it back in the bank was a daring plot. When Frank reached the end, Dad's face was lit up.

"It's **brilliant,** mate!"

"Thanks, Dad." The boy beamed with pride.

"Just one problem."

"What?"

"We need a set of wheels to carry out this plan of yours."

"Queenie?"

"We need her now more than ever."

"Will she still be in the field where we left her?"

"No, no, no. The fuzz will have towed her away by now."

"Where will she be, then?"

"They will have sold the old girl off for scrap."

"Scrap?!"

"I know, but there's life in the old girl yet. I am just praying we get to her in time."

"Me too."

"As soon as we've got home and I've changed out of this dress…"

"I dunno, Dad. It kinda suits you," joked Frank.

"Very funny, mate. Come on, this is our stop!"

The scrapyard was like a graveyard for cars. Most looked beyond repair, with their crushed bonnets, missing wheels and bodies brown with rust.

A huge crane towered overhead, picking up cars by their roofs with a giant claw. Then it hoisted them through the air before dropping them into a giant crushing machine. This could squeeze any car, however big, into a brick the size of a microwave oven.

Finding **Queenie** among the hundreds of wrecks was not going to be easy, but they desperately needed her. The Mini had been a part of Frank and his father's lives for so long that she seemed like a member of the family. As they searched the scrapyard, the boy called the car's name out loud.

"Queenie?"

"Ha! Ha! She's not a dog, but it might just work!" said Dad before joining in. "Queenie?"

"Queenie?"

"Queenie?"

"Queenie?"

As they paced the rows and rows of wrecks, Frank noticed many of them were police cars, no doubt destroyed by the pair's last escapade. He was too distracted to notice that something strange was going on with the crane. It was slowly rumbling closer and closer towards them. Now dangling right over their heads was a huge old Bentley that must have weighed a ton. A shadow fell across them. Frank realised it was suddenly colder and darker.

At that moment the crane released its claw. In the blink of an eye, the huge Bentley was falling through the air.

"LOOK OUT!" shouted Dad as he pushed his son away.

*BOOM!*

The Bentley smashed on to the ground, trapping Dad's leg underneath. The man remained remarkably calm.

"*Dad!* Why aren't you screaming?"

"It's my wooden leg! That's the one that doesn't hurt."

"I have to get you out."

Using all his strength, the boy pulled his father from under the car.

"How is the leg?" asked Frank.

Dad examined it. "A few cracks and splinters. I can always get another one!"

Frank could feel the air whooshing around them. He looked up to see the crane's claw coming straight for them.

# "DAD!"

The pair rolled out of the way, and the claw dug into the ground.

## BOOF!

"Who is driving that thing?" asked the boy.

Dad looked up to catch sight of the man in the crane's cab. He knew that **DEVILISH** smirk anywhere. It was Fingers.

"Thumbs must have worked it out and told Fingers," said Dad. "They're on to us!"

"Let's run!" said Frank.

"We need to find **Queenie** first!"

The pair scrambled to their feet, and raced off round the corner, the crane's claw swooping down on them.

"There she is!" exclaimed Frank. He'd spotted their old girl's bonnet poking out from a long row of wrecks. **Queenie** did not look her best, crumpled from crashing into a tree and with the yellow paint half washed off by the rain. The windscreen was smashed, the headlamps were cracked and her roof had been bashed in. Frank and his father raced towards the old girl.

"It's good to be home," said Dad as he slid into the driving seat, and turned the key that had been left in the ignition.

# ROAR!

The engine roared like old times.

"Let's go!" said Dad, and the car zoomed off through the scrapyard.

# BANG!

Frank looked up. The crane's claw had smashed through the roof of the car. With ease, the crane picked up the Mini.

# "NOOO!" screamed the boy as the little

car swung through the air like a conker.

# WHOOP!

In seconds, Frank and Dad were dangling over the crushing machine, with its terrifying metal mouth gaping wide. They could make out Fingers in the crane's cab, laughing like a hyena.

"SWING FORWARD, SON!" shouted Dad.

The pair threw their weight forward just as the claw opened to drop the car.

"HOLD TIGHT!" said Dad.

*WHOOSH!*

The car fell through the air.

"ARGH!" screamed the boy.

# CHAPTER 52

# CRUSHER

**Queenie** landed on the rim of the crusher.

*THUⁿK!*

She wobbled there, Frank and his father hanging between life and death.

"Swing forward again!" cried Dad. They both swung forward and the car slid off the rim of the crusher and hit the ground.

*THUD!*

Dad then pressed hard on the accelerator. But no sooner had **Queenie** sped forward than the crane's claw smashed through what was left of the roof.

"HOLD ON!" said Dad to his son. The man did a handbrake turn, putting the car into a **wild spin.**

The claw tore the roof clean off **Queenie**. It was like peeling open a tin of sardines.

"I always wanted **Queenie** to have a sunroof," said Dad as the car smashed through a wire fence…

*THWACK!*

…and sped out of the scrapyard.

*ROAR!*

Still the crane thundered after them, its caterpillar tracks whirring as it gave chase.

Ahead was a sign that read **"LOW BRIDGE"**. The pair smiled at each other as they raced past it. **Queenie** zoomed under the bridge. Frank climbed up out of his seat and looked behind out of the brand-new sunroof. The crane was way too tall. It smashed straight into the bridge.

**DOOF!**

Bricks exploded everywhere.

# KABOOM!

LOW BRIDGE

Like a staggering *Tyrannosaurus rex*, the crane
ground to a halt.
## BASH!

In the distance, Frank could see Fingers leap out of the cab, kick the ailing crane with his foot and then wince at the pain.

"**First stop, Mr Big's!**" shouted the boy over the roar of the Mini's engine.

*ROAR!*

# CHAPTER

# 53

# DEEP, DARK DREAD

The pair of bank un-robbers hid **Queenie** in a hedgerow before making the final part of the journey to Mr Big's country house on foot. It was late now, and all they could hear were their own footsteps echoing on the wet road.

Frank felt frightened, but didn't want to admit it.

"Let me hold your hand, Dad. I just don't want you to trip over," he lied.

"Thanks, mate," replied the man, looking scared too.

Pilfer House was surrounded by a huge stone wall.

"Please can I borrow your leg?" asked the boy.

"I will need it back."

"Yeah, yeah, of course, Dad!"

As soon as the man had taken off his wooden leg, Frank turned it upside down and used the foot as a hook on the stone wall. Next he hoisted himself up.

Once he was standing on top of the wall, Frank lowered the leg to pull his father up. Both then leaped into the grand garden below. From that safe distance, Frank studied the house.

"If I remember right, Big's study must be that room with the huge window there. Follow me," said the boy with confidence.

"Just one thing, mate."

"Yes, Dad?"

"Please can I have my leg back?"

"Oops!" said the boy.

As soon as Dad had reattached it, they were on their way.

It came as no surprise to discover that all the windows and doors to Pilfer House were locked. Mr Big had become *rich* by stealing from others, but no one would be allowed to steal from him.

"Locked, locked, locked!" cursed Dad.

"Maybe I could borrow your leg again?"

"What for this time?"

"To break a window?" suggested the boy.

"That will wake everyone up, mate."

Frank thought for a moment. "Dad, Big has got those two huge cats, remember?"

"Yeah! Horrible creatures called Ronnie and Reggie. So...?"

"So there must be a catflap! Maybe I am small enough to squeeze through it."

"It's worth a try!"

Round the back of the house, Frank found the small hatch at the bottom of the kitchen door.

"I'm not sure about this, mate," said Dad. "There's locks on the inside of all the windows. I won't be able to get in. You'll be on your own in Big's house. It's dangerous."

"I'm not scared," lied the boy. "From out here you can see if any lights come on in the house and warn me."

"All right, but how are you going to get into the safe?"

"I memorised the tune the butler made when he pressed the code in. BEEP! BOOP! BLEEP! BLOOP!"

"You've thought of everything. All right, in you go, but, mate…"

"Yes, Dad?"

"Be careful."

The boy nodded, and ducked down on to his hands

and knees. It was a tight squeeze but he just made it through the cat flap.

FLIP!
FLAP!

Once inside the house, a deep, dark dread descended upon the boy. Here he was, alone in the dark inside the home of a master criminal, about to steal half a million pounds from him. It couldn't be more dangerous.

As he crawled across the kitchen floor, Frank could hear snoring.

"ZZZZ! ZZZZ!"

The boy glanced over to the basket in the corner.

Ronnie and Reggie were curled up together, sleeping. Frank tiptoed past them out into the corridor. This was longer than a football pitch, with doors dotted along either side. Which one was the study door? Suddenly Frank felt sick to his stomach, as he realised he didn't have a clue. Now he had no idea if he had come too far, or not far enough.

Frank tried a few handles, and found they were all locked. Eventually he discovered one that wasn't. The boy opened the door as slowly and quietly as he could. Inside the room, darkness reigned, save for a dot of red light. The boy felt something stinging his eyes and burning the back of his throat. The red light glowed. It was the end of a cigar.

A table lamp flicked on, **blazing** straight into the boy's eyes.

As he blinked at the brightness, a voice said, **"Well, if it isn't the little thief. I've been expecting you."**

It was Mr Big.

# CHAPTER

**54**

# LIAR

"I am impressed, young Frank," began the **master criminal**. "Breaking into my house in the dead of night. You are a boy after my own heart. You need to come and live here with me and your mother. I could be the father you never had. I could train you up. Teach you everything I know. You could become a **master criminal** like me. One day all this could be yours."

"I don't want it," snapped the boy. "I don't want any of it."

"Of course you do," chuckled Big. "This is everyone's dream. Just think, your own swimming pool, servants. You can even race my fleet of supercars around the grounds. Join me..." said the man as he reached out his hand.

# "NO! NEVER!"

"No one says no to Mr Big."

"Everything you have is built on hurting others. You know what? You aren't half the man my dad is."

"Is that so?" Mr Big leaned forward. "Which reminds me, where is that pathetic excuse for a human being?"

The boy could just make out his father standing outside the window right behind Mr Big. Frank didn't dare let his eyes drift over or he would give the game away.

"He's in prison, of course. He doesn't know anything about me being here tonight."

Mr Big chuckled to himself. "Ha! Ha! A liar as well as a thief."

"I am not a liar!"

The man got up out of his seat, not that it made much difference to his height. He shone a lamp into the boy's face.

"Thumbs takes his nephews to visit his brothers in the nick, says he sees something fishy as you are leaving. Fingers is waiting outside in the motor, and follows you to the scrapyard. There, you go to get your crummy little car back. Why? What is your plan, my son?"

"I am not your son!"

"Tell me," purred Big.

"NO!" shouted the boy.

Mr Big smiled to himself. The evil little man was clearly getting a kick out of upsetting the boy like this. "Come on. Daddy needs to know what his little thief is up to now..."

"YOU ARE NOT AND NEVER

WILL BE MY DADDY! AND I AM NOT A THIEF!" exclaimed the boy, his eyes stinging with tears. "If you must know, I am going to steal the money and put it back in the bank."

Mr Big hooted with laughter. "Ha! Ha! Ha! We got there. Finally!"

"Darn!" said Frank. He'd given his masterplan away.

"In all my years, I've never heard anything so stupid! I'm not sure you're all there," said the man, prodding the boy's head with his short, stubby fingers. "You're not working alone, though, are you, boy? For the last time, where is that one-legged father of yours?"

Mr Big took a long drag from his cigar, and blew the thick, black smoke straight into the boy's face. Frank coughed and spluttered. Out of the corner of his eye, he could see his father was taking off his wooden leg.

"I told you – I don't know," replied Frank.

Mr Big shook his head slowly. He took the cigar out of his mouth, and held the red-hot glowing end close to the boy's nose. "I've been nice. Now it's time to get nasty."

Slowly he moved the cigar closer and closer. Frank couldn't help it – his eyes flickered over to Dad. Mr Big turned round to see the man hopping around outside the window. Above his head he was brandishing his wooden leg.

"What the…?" exclaimed Mr Big.

# CHAPTER

## 55

# WRINKLY BOTTOM

Before Mr Big could utter another word, Dad's false

leg crashed down through the window…

…and the wooden foot bashed Mr Big hard on the

head.

## $BON_K!$

The crime boss collapsed

to the floor, out cold.

### THUD!

"Someone will have heard that," said Dad, bashing the bits of broken glass out of the window with his fake foot so he could climb through it.

"Thanks for saving my skin, Dad."

"My pleasure! I've been wanting to knock out that nasty piece of work for years." Dad looked down at the little man sprawled on his silk rug. "Now come on, mate, we don't have much time."

"I'll be as quick as I can." The boy rushed to the oil painting of Mr Big hanging on the wall. He pulled it to one side to reveal the electronic keypad to the safe.

**"*BEEP! BOOP! BLEEP! BLOOP!*"** he said to himself, remembering the noise the buttons made when he'd seen it opened. He pressed a few of the numbers as if they were piano keys, trying to hear the right notes.

**_BOOP! BEEP!_**

He needed to remember which number made what sound.

**_BLOOP! BOOP!_**

Just as he felt he was getting closer, the door to the study creaked open. Chang the elderly butler entered, wearing only a pair of skimpy black underpants. He circled Dad and Frank, chanting something in Mandarin with his arms outstretched, as if about to do kung fu. Chang took a few steps backwards to get a run-up, and then jumped. The old man flew through the air with his arms and legs flung out.

Frank ducked out of the way. Dad helpfully opened a window and Chang flew right through it…

## WHOOSH!

…landing on the patio outside with a

## THUD!

Frank and his father peered out of the open window at the butler lying face down on the ground.

"He knocked himself out," said Dad.

The skimpy black underpants had ridden up, and now Chang's wrinkly old bottom was pointing in their direction.

"He needs to buy himself some pyjamas," muttered

Frank, before going back to work on the safe.

*BEEP! BOOP! BLEEP! BLOOP! CLICK!*

He'd cracked the code! The safe door whirred open.

"YES!" exclaimed the boy.

Father and son stared into the safe. For a moment, neither said a word. There was more money in that little metal box than they could ever dream of. There was far too much to count, but it was in the millions, if not tens of millions.

"Why don't we just take the lot?" asked Dad. "We could run away, buy a big yacht, sail around the world forever."

The thought was tempting. The money looked like the answer to everything.

"I don't know, Dad," replied the boy. "If we took the lot, we'd be as bad as Big down there. Let's take what was robbed from the bank, and not a penny more."

The boy started counting the bundles and putting them in the bin liner they'd brought.

Dad shook his head in disbelief, and pleaded with his son. "Can't we just take a tiny bit more for us?"

"What kind of dad do you want to be, a good dad or a **bad dad?**"

The man pondered this for a moment. "Is there something in the middle?"

"No!"

"A good dad, then!"

"I knew it," said the boy.

"You go ahead and check the coast is clear."

Frank did as he was told, and poked his head out of the broken window.

"Dad?"

"What?" said the man.

"Come and see."

Dad joined him at the window. Outside on the patio was a figure framed in the broken glass. It was Mum. And she was holding a gun.

# CHAPTER 56

# MUM WITH A GUN

"Don't do anything stupid, Rita!" pleaded Dad.

In her hands was a pistol, which she pointed straight at him.

"I thought you were **rotting** away in prison," she purred.

"I was," replied Dad. "But I am out, just for the night."

Mum approached the broken window and peered inside.

"What have you done to my Biggie?" she demanded on seeing her boyfriend sprawled out on his silk rug.

"I knocked him out with my wooden leg," answered Dad.

"I bet you enjoyed that, Gilbert," she snarled.

"Do you know what, Rita? I did."

"I can't believe all those years ago I fell in love with you," she said.

"I can believe I was in love with you," replied Dad. "But you were different then, Rita. Before Mr Big came along and turned your head with his *riches*."

"Biggie knows how to treat a lady."

"Love isn't measured in *gold* and **diamonds**. That man down there doesn't love you. You're just another one of his *possessions*."

Mum cocked the pistol, ready to fire.

CLICK!

"I've had quite enough of listening to you, Gilbert. Now get out of my house. But leave the boy with me."

Frank felt a wave of panic crash over him. Living in this huge house with his mum and her boyfriend was the last thing he wanted.

"I know you're angry with me for walking out, Frank," said Mum. "But I want you back in my life."

Dad looked to his son. "What do *you* want, Frank?"

"I bet you want to come and live here in this big house in the lap of luxury with me and Biggie, don't you?"

"NO," replied the boy in a flash.

Instantly the woman crumbled in front of his eyes. "What do you mean 'no'?"

"I'm sorry, Mum, but I don't want to live here with you. Not ever. All I want is to be with my dad."

"Even though he's got nothing? In fact, *less* than nothing," she said.

"Dad's got everything I need and more," replied Frank. "And he doesn't have to point a gun at anyone to make me love him."

Deep sorrow crept across Mum's face and she burst

into tears. Trembling, she brought the gun down and sank to her knees.

"I am so, so sorry, Frank. I took a wrong turn in life. I made a mistake walking out, but I've had to live with it. I know I let you down, Frank. I bet you hate my guts."

The boy stepped through the glass window and joined her on the patio. Slowly he approached his mother, and wrapped his arms round her. "I don't hate you, Mum. I love you."

These three words made her sob even more.

"Please forgive me, Frank," she said through tears. "I should have been a mother to you. I've been lost. So lost. But, son, I realise now what a fool I've been. I love you too."

"I forgive you, Mum."

Mum held her son tightly as Dad stepped through the broken window to stand beside them. After a few moments, the boy eased himself away from his mother.

"I'm sorry, but me and Dad have to go," said Frank.

Mum tried to sniff back the tears. "Where are you two going at this time of night?"

"We have to right a wrong, Mum. A big wrong."

Mum nodded her head. "You've always got to right a wrong."

# CHAPTER

57

# FEARSOME BEASTS

Frank took his mother by the arm. "It's cold, Mum. Let me get you back inside."

Gilbert watched his son with pride who, despite everything, was showing his mother such kindness.

Frank looked back at her through the broken window. There was his mother standing alone in the study in her silk nightdress, tears running down her face, with mascara smudged around her eyes.

The boy took his father's hand, and they stepped off the patio into the garden.

"We have to come back for her," said Frank.

"We'll see," replied Dad.

As the pair reached the stone wall that surrounded

Mr Big's house, two **fearsome beasts** jumped down from a tree and landed on their heads.

"AARGH!" they screamed.

It was Ronnie and Reggie, the world's most terrifyingly big small cats.

"Get off!" screamed Dad as Ronnie leaped on to his back, digging his sharp claws into his chest.

"Help!" screamed Frank as Reggie leaped on to his head and punched him square on the nose with his paw.

"Dad! I can't pull him off!" screamed Frank.

"Nor me!" said Dad as he desperately tried to yank the cat off his back. The animal's claws had gone deep into the man's flesh. "But I know there's one thing cats really hate!"

"What?" asked the boy as Reggie rained more blows down upon him.

"WATER!"

"The fountain!" exclaimed Frank, and they ran off in the direction of it.

"Oh no!" exclaimed the boy as they sprinted. "His bum is in my face!"

"**Keep running!**" said Dad even as Ronnie bit into his ear with his fangs. "OUCH!"

The pair held hands as they leaped into the fountain.

SPLOSH!

Instead of being scared by water, the two cats turned out to be expert swimmers. They dived into the pond and, like jet-propelled sharks, pursued the father and son round and round the fountain.

"Jump out!" shouted Dad.

As the pair scrambled across the gravel, Ronnie and Reggie gave chase. In a panic, Frank slipped and fell flat on his face. Gilbert kneeled down to help him up.

"MEOW!" screamed the cats as they leaped through the air and landed on the pair's backs.

They pinned them down, sinking their claws deeper and deeper into Frank and Dad's flesh.

"ARGH!" screamed Frank.

"We're done for!" said Dad.

But then, "HISS!" hissed the cats as they were yanked off father and son.

Frank looked up. His mother had grabbed both animals by their tails.

"MUM!" exclaimed the boy.

"I always hated these cats!" she said. Then she spun round and round as if she was a champion disco dancer, gripping on to a tail in each hand.

"HISS!" hissed the cats. They didn't like it one bit.

When she was going so fast that Ronnie and Reggie were just a blur, she let go.

"MMMEEEOOOWWW!!!" screamed the cats as they sailed through the air, landing with two loud thuds in a distant corner of the garden.

# BOOF!
# BOOF!

"Thank you, Rita," said Dad.

"Don't worry," she said. "Now go, before Big wakes up!"

"Thank you, Mum," said Frank.

"I'm glad to help you two, even just a little bit," replied Mum. "Be careful."

"We will," lied Frank.

"RITA!" came a voice from inside the house.

"GO! GO! GO!" she urged.

In seconds they were gone.

# CHAPTER 58

# KILL TWO BIRDS
# WITH ONE STONE

Once on the other side of the Pilfer House wall, the pair found **Queenie**, slung the money on the back seat and sped off in the direction of the bank. It was well past midnight now, and there was no one about. Dad stopped the car in a side road opposite the bank, and turned off the headlights.

A couple of months had passed since the robbery, and the bank had been repaired.

"How are we going to break in?" asked Dad.

"I don't think we should blow it up again," replied Frank. "There's no point creating a **million pounds'** worth of damage to put half a **million pounds** back in the vault."

"No," muttered Dad. "It would be fun, though."

"This is the plan I worked out, Dad. We're going to wait until the first person arrives for work at the bank, and then trick our way in."

"That could be hours."

"No. One morning I got up really early and sneaked out of Auntie Flip's house to watch the bank. The bank manager arrives each morning at dawn."

"Good work. Let's just sit tight until then, and we can trick our way in."

At that moment the crane from the scrapyard tr**u**n**d**led round the corner. Fingers was once again at the controls. It stopped right outside the bank and Fingers jumped to the ground. Behind it was one of Mr Big's Rolls-Royces. Thumbs stepped out of the fancy car and opened the door for his boss. Mr Big emerged, nursing his battered head with a bag of ice.

"Those two rats are in there somewhere! I know it," he said to his henchmen. "They are putting my hard-stolen money back in the bank."

**"Disgusting!"** said Thumbs.

"It's just not right," added Fingers.

"Let's sneak out of the car before they spot us," whispered Dad.

The pair slid down from their seats, and crawled along the street on their hands and knees, taking the bin liner full of money with them. They found a hiding place behind a postbox.

"Look, guv'nor! It's a Mini just like theirs!" announced Thumbs.

"It *is* their Mini!" said Fingers.

"Well done, Thumbs. You get a gold star."

Mr Big crossed the road, his silk dressing gown blowing in the wind. He peered into **Queenie** through the large hole in her roof.

"They're not in the car! So I was right. They must be inside the bank already," he said. Mr Big crossed back over the road and rattled the doors to the bank. "Clever! They must have barricaded themselves in. Fingers! DO YOUR WORST!"

"Right away, guv'nor!" replied Fingers with a grin. "A little demolition job."

"Yes, we can kill two birds with one stone."

"I don't think there are any birds we need to kill, guv'nor," said Thumbs.

"Oh, do shut up or I'll order you to punch yourself!"

Fingers drove the crane towards the Mini. Its thick metal arm swung through the air, and its claw picked up **Queenie** with ease.

C*LAN*K*!*

Then the arm swung again, and the little car reeled

towards the bank. Frank held tightly on to his dad's arm. The man closed his eyes. He couldn't watch what was about to happen.

## CRASH!

**Queenie** smashed through the entrance to the bank.

## BOOM!

The doors and windows burst on to the street.

## CRASH!

The bank's alarm blared.

## RING!

The crane swung back to reveal a crumpled mess that used to be **Queenie**. The whole front end of the car had been destroyed. The grille had dropped off, the bonnet had been bashed and the front wheels were dangling by a thread.

"No!" whispered Dad. The poor man had tears in his eyes.

"I'm so sorry, Dad," whispered the boy. He put his arm round his father. "I know you loved her."

"Farewell, Your Majesty," said Dad.

"FINISH HER OFF!" ordered Mr Big.

"Yes, sir," replied Fingers. He pulled a lever on the crane and hoisted the car as high as it would go.

*WHIRR!*

It swayed in the wind for a few moments. Then the claw opened and the Mini fell through the air.

*WHIZZ!*

In a second it hit the road.

*BOOM!*

The crane then surged forward, and crushed what was left of the car under its caterpillar tracks.

*WHIRR!*
*CRUNCH!*

**Queenie** had been a member of the family for as long as Frank could remember. Now she was nothing more than a flattened mess of metal.

"That's their getaway car knackered, guv'nor," said Fingers with a wicked grin.

"Good work, Fingers. Now I want my money

back. Let's get in there and stop those two rats before the filth arrive," ordered Mr Big, and he followed his henchmen inside the bank.

"What are we going to do, mate?" asked Dad.

"Kill two birds with one stone," replied the boy.

Father gave son a puzzled look.

"You'll see," said Frank, pulling his dad along.

# CHAPTER 59

## OVERCOOKED SAUSAGES

Without realising it, Mr Big and his goon squad were doing most of the hard work for Frank and Dad. Father and son were now able to waltz straight into the bank. The only trouble was that the alarm had been set off and the police were sure to arrive in moments. Working fast, they followed the path of destruction left by the three criminals down to the bank's vault. Doors had been **smashed** off hinges, glass **broken** and electronic keypads **bashed** in.

# KABOOM!

Frank and his father were rocked by an **explosion.** Debris fell from the ceiling, a cloud of black smoke filled the air and any windows that hadn't already been broken exploded, spraying bullets of glass everywhere. The pair covered their faces with their hands.

"Are you all right, mate?" spluttered Dad as he gasped for air.

"Fine. I think. Let's carry on."

Together they stumbled forward, and stopped at the top of a spiral staircase.

"The vault must be down in the basement," whispered Dad.

The pair tiptoed down the stairs. The smoke cleared to reveal an amusing sight. The criminal gang had clearly used far too much dynamite to blow the lock on the door to the vault. All three were singed, burnt black with smoke snaking off them. Mr Big, Fingers and Thumbs looked like three sausages that had been overcooked on a barbecue.

"There they are!" said Fingers, pointing with his long, thin, charred finger.

Thumbs looked mightily confused. "But we thought you were in the vault already."

"Well, you were wrong! We were out here the whole time," said Frank with a grin.

"Oh," replied the henchman, bowing his head.

Mr Big rocked uneasily in his slippers. From the look on his face he loathed being outsmarted like this. "Actually, you two have fallen straight into my trap!"

"How is that, then, Biggie?" asked Dad.

"Well, erm, because, well…" the man stumbled, "because now we are going to steal back the money from you that we stole from the bank, and steal some more! And you two idiots are going to get the blame! Fingers, Thumbs, take it all. Every last penny!"

"Me bag's got a hole in it now," said Thumbs.

"Mine's got two," added Fingers.

Just like their clothes, the dynamite had taken its toll on the bags.

"Well then, stuff your pockets!" ordered Mr Big.

The two henchmen examined what was left of their coats.

"Not got any pockets no more," replied Thumbs.

"I've got one, guv'nor!" said Fingers. "Oh no, sorry. It's got a hole in it," he added, wiggling one of his fingers through to demonstrate.

"You can borrow our bag," said Frank.

"But that's got **half a million quid** in it, mate," hissed Dad out of the corner of his mouth so only his son could hear.

## "Bring it to me, boy," ordered Big.

The boy took a few paces forward, and handed the bag to Mr Big. The little man looked inside, and his face lit up.

"**Ah! My babies.** Oh, how I missed you," he said, before passing the bin liner to Fingers.

Then the two henchmen disappeared inside the vault, and began **stuffing** the bag with wad after wad of money. Frank peered into the vault to get a better look.

"Look at all that lovely money,

boy," said Big. "More money than you could ever earn in a lifetime. Just there for the taking."

The boy's eyes **widened**.

"I know you're tempted, boy. Look at it. It can give you anything you want. Anything."

Frank stared at it, mesmerised. "It's… beautiful."

"It is," replied Mr Big, egging the boy on. "Money is the most beautiful thing in the world."

"I love it," said Frank. It was as if his eyes had lit up with gold. "I love, love, love it."

"But, mate?" pleaded Dad. "Think! What are you doing?"

"Come with me, boy," continued Mr Big. He stretched out his hand towards the boy. "Take your rightful place at my side. I can be the father you never had. Join me. Together we can rule the world."

Frank took a deep breath. "I would like that," he said. "I would like that very much."

Poor Dad had tears in his eyes. "MATE! NO-OO!"

"I'm so pleased you've come round to my way of thinking, boy," said Mr Big, shooting a smug look at Gilbert.

"Let's start right now," said Frank. He took Mr Big's hand, and led the man into the vault.

"MATE!" screamed Dad.

As if in a trance, the boy kept going further and further inside.

Mr Big turned back to Gilbert and smirked. "You've lost, little man."

# CHAPTER

## 60

# FURY

As Big and his goons busied themselves greedily stuffing the bag full of more and more money, the boy slowly backed out of the vault. Once he'd passed the thick metal door, he whispered, **"Dad! I tricked them! Help me!"**

"Clever boy!"

The boy began pushing the door shut. Dad rushed to help, and together they used all their strength to try to close it. Inside the vault Big looked up.

**"GET THE DOOR!"** he shouted, and he and his gang ran towards it. They smashed

their shoulders up against the door, pushing with all their might, desperate not to be trapped inside.

"I knew you wouldn't let me down," said Dad.

"Never!" replied the boy as they both strained against the door.

Mr Big just managed to squeeze his face through the tiny gap.

"You are no match for me, Gilbert," said the man. "I pity you. No wife. No money. No leg. The plan was for you to die in that little racing 'accident'."

"You made that happen?" said Dad, shaking with fury.

"I wanted Rita. And I wanted you out of the way. Forever."

"I booby-trapped your engine," shouted Fingers.

"And I cut your brakes," screamed Thumbs. "But your plan didn't work, did it?" replied Dad defiantly. "Because I'm still here!"

"You are right," agreed Mr Big. "But you know what? I think I prefer you crippled. That way, I've had the pleasure of watching you suffer all these years."

"NOT ANY MORE!" yelled Dad.

"NOW IT'S YOUR TURN TO SUFFER!" shouted Frank.

The anger made the pair strong. Together they just managed to push the three back and slam the vault door behind them.

*CL<sup>UN</sup>K!*

But they couldn't lock it!

"Darn!" said Dad. "Look! They've blown the bolt on the door."

"We need to jam them in somehow," said Frank. "Let's put that thing to one final good use."

"What thing?"

"That leg of yours!"

"I can't leave it here!"

"Dad! We have no choice!"

Reluctantly, the man whipped his wooden leg off and together they slid it into place. The door was blocked. Faintly they could hear the three criminals pounding on the other side, pathetically pleading for mercy.

"We can make a deal!"

"It was all Fingers's idea."

"Thumbs made me do it."

Frank and his father looked at each other and smiled.

"See, Dad. We killed two birds with one stone. We put the money back and trapped the real criminals in there at the same time!"

"You, mate, are a genius!" exclaimed Dad.

"Thank you, Dad."

"The police will find them. In no time at all. In fact, we need to get out of here. NOW!" Without needing to say another word, he put his arm over his son's shoulders for support. Frank helped his dad hop up the spiral staircase.

As they reached the entrance to the bank, dawn was breaking. In the distance, they could hear police sirens **wailing.**

*NEE-NAW! NEE-NAW! NEE-NAW!*

They rushed the other way down the street.

"Right! Now back to prison for you, Dad!" said Frank.

# CHAPTER

# 61

# THE NOISE! THE PEOPLE!

Once Dad had hopped all the way home, he changed himself back into Auntie Flip's long, *flowery* dress. Without his wooden leg, the man was struggling to get around. So Frank hurriedly improvised a new one from an old plastic mop in the kitchen. The pair jumped on the bus to take them to **Wrongfoot Prison** at the far side of the town. It wasn't visiting day until next week, so they were going to have to blag their way in somehow.

Frank's idea was that they should say they had some upsetting news to tell Gilbert Goodie. The pair would make up a distant relative – a cousin or uncle or someone – and say that they'd died and had to tell the boy's father in person.

"Who goes there?" barked Mr Swivel through a tiny hatch at the huge metal front door of **Wrongfoot Prison**.

"Gilbert Goodie is my father and I have some very sad news for him," blubbed Frank. He'd made himself cry by hiding a raw onion in a tissue, and dabbing his eyes with it.

Dad, dressed as Auntie Flip, put a comforting arm round the boy's shoulder. "Oh, it's you!" exclaimed Swivel. "You were here only yesterday. We are closed to visitors for two weeks. What is this SAD news, exactly?" demanded the prison guard.

"It better be really, really, really gut-wrenchingly sad."

"I don't know how to say this without breaking down, but…" began Frank.

"GET ON WITH IT, BOY!" ordered Mr Swivel.

"…his Uncle Keith has passed away," blubbed Dad.

"Dead?" asked Mr Swivel.

"Yes," replied Dad.

"Completely dead?"

"Yes. One hundred per cent completely, utterly, never-going-to-be-alive-again dead."

"I'll tell him!" snapped Mr Swivel. With that, he slid the metal hatch shut.

Frank and his dad looked at each other in panic. This was not part of the plan.

"WE NEED TO TELL GILBERT FACE TO FACE!" shouted Dad through the prison door.

"WHY?" shouted Mr Swivel from the other side.

"Erm, because we wouldn't want you to spoil the surprise!" replied Frank.

Dad looked at his son as if to say, "What are you on about?!"

"Surprise?" said Swivel.

"Yes. He always hated Uncle Keith!" replied Frank.

There was the sound of keys jangling, and then the huge metal door slid open.

*CL*$^{UNK!}$

"You've got two minutes. I've got my eye on you," said the prison guard, though he didn't state which eye, the real one or the glass one.

Mr Swivel took the two up to a little grey room and told them to wait. Moments later, he led in Auntie Flip, dressed as Dad. The poor woman looked completely frazzled after her night in the cells.

"They've got some news for you," barked the prison guard. "Your Uncle Keith has snuffed it."

"Who?" replied Auntie Flip.

"You know – Uncle Keith," continued Dad, winking at the lady and hoping she might realise this was a scam. "Your uncle who you knew very well."

"Oh, old Uncle Keith! Yes, of course I remember!" exclaimed Auntie Flip. "How is he?"

"Dead," replied Frank.

"*DEAD?* NOOOOOOO!" screamed the lady, and she burst into a fountain of tears.

The prison guard observed all this like a hawk. A one-eyed hawk.

"You said your father always hated Uncle Keith," said Mr Swivel.

"Yes, well, hate is a strong word, yes, but you always disliked him, Dad. Remember?" prompted the boy.

The lady eventually got the hint, and began hooting with fake laughter. "Ho! Ho! Uncle Keith has kicked the bucket. Yippee!"

Mr Swivel shook his head, mightily confused by this bizarre family. "Right, get out of my prison, you two weirdos," he barked.

"Could we have a moment to grieve as a family in peace, Mr Swivel?" pleaded Dad as Auntie Flip.

"Grieve?" asked Mr Swivel.

"I mean celebrate," said Dad.

The prison guard sighed. "All right, all right, you have one minute, and not a second more!" he barked, slamming the door behind him.

## *BANG!*

"We'd better swap clothes quickly," said Dad.

"Yes, I can't wait to get out of here," replied the lady.

"Did you not enjoy your night in prison, Auntie Flip?" asked the boy.

The lady looked at Frank as if he was stark raving mad.

"The noise! The people!" she exclaimed. "I had to share a cell with these six brutes who were brothers.

I couldn't sleep a wink. They were all staring at me funny. I thought they were on to me. That they might do me in during the night. But I began reciting some of my poetry about the joys of garden centres to them and that sent them all off to sleep in an instant."

"I bet," murmured Frank under his breath.

"Now, boy, close your eyes while we get changed."

Frank did what he was told.

In a few moments, Auntie Flip announced, "Right, you can open them again!"

Frank opened his eyes, relieved to see that Dad was back to being Dad, and Auntie Flip was back to being Auntie Flip.

"I am me again. Thank the Lord!" said the lady, lifting her hands in prayer.

## CL*IC*K!

At that moment, Mr Swivel marched back into the room. "Right, that's quite enough crying or laughing or whatever bizarre thing you do in this family when someone snuffs it. You two, out!"

Auntie Flip and Frank were led out of the room. As he reached the door, the boy looked over his shoulder and smiled at his father.

"**OUT!**" barked Mr Swivel.

# 62

# GOTCHA, GANGSTA!

Reluctantly, Frank had to leave his father in prison as he and Auntie Flip returned to her house. The boy was sure it would only be a matter of time until the news came out of what had happened at the bank. Sure enough, a visit to Raj's shop the next morning brought good news.

# *DING!*

"Frank! Have you seen the morning newspapers? LOOK! The police have finally arrested that nasty gang who've been terrorising this town for years!"

"Let me see, Raj!"

The boy hungrily read the headlines.

"They have to let my dad out of prison now!" exclaimed the boy.

"Why?" asked Raj.

"These men must be the real baddies!"

The newsagent pondered this for a moment. "Well, your father couldn't have been part of last night's bank robbery as he has the perfect alibi. He was in prison the whole time!"

"Of course!" exclaimed the boy, not wishing to give the game away. "And the money that was stolen from the robbery before got put back in the vault anyway!"

This stopped Raj in his tracks. "How do you know that?"

"What?" asked Frank.

"How do you know that? I read all the newspapers. Not one of them said that."

The boy became flustered. "I… er, well, um, I…"

Raj's eyes widened. "Young man, you are not telling me that you had something to do with all this…?"

Frank thought it better to keep his masterplan secret. "Raj, I have to go."

"Where?"

"Court! I have to try to get my dad out of prison!"

"This I have to see!" replied the newsagent, and the pair dashed out of the shop.

# DING!

# CHAPTER 63

# ROTTEN FRUIT

That afternoon, Auntie Flip and Frank weaved their way through the huge crowds outside the court, and just managed to find two seats upstairs in the gallery. It was jammed full of people desperate to see Mr Big and his henchmen finally in the dock. There were rows of journalists, clutching their notebooks and pencils, eager to write down every detail of the trial to splash over tomorrow's front pages. However, they were outnumbered by some of the townsfolk whom the criminal gang had terrorised over the years, all chattering to each other excitedly.

*"At last they got the little bully!"*

**"I hope that nasty so-and-so gets sent away forever!"**

"Those two hyenas of his are just as bad!"

"WHOEVER HAS DONE THIS DESERVES A MEDAL!"

*"This is the best day our town has seen in years!"*

Auntie Flip and Frank listened, and shared a secret smile.

Everyone in the courtroom stood as Judge Pillar shuffled in. He took his place on his throne and banged his gavel on his desk.

"Bring in the accused."

Mr Big, Fingers and Thumbs were all led in by policemen. Their hands were cuffed, and they were still wearing their charred clothes from the night before. On seeing them, the court erupted. The townsfolk had been concealing rotten fruit under their coats, and hurled it at the three criminals.

*WHIZZ!*

"TAKE THAT!" shouted the old lady from the church with the hearing aid as she threw a watermelon. *SPLAT!*

It burst on Mr Big's head, spraying watermelon juice everywhere.

A tiny man in a neck brace threw a pineapple, which hit Thumbs on the nose.

# BONK!

"OW!" shouted the henchman.

"GET A TASTE OF YOUR OWN MEDICINE!" yelled the tiny man as cheers erupted in the court.

## "HOORAY!"

If Fingers was feeling smug to be the only one not to have been hit, that was soon to change. A lady in a wheelchair pulled out a catapult and fired a bag of tomatoes at the man. One by one they exploded on to Fingers's face.

## SPLURGE! SPLURGE! SPLURGE!

"GOTCHA! GOTCHA! GOTCHA!" shouted the lady.

"Stop!" yelled Fingers through his tears.

The judge, who'd been transfixed by what was going on, finally reached for his gavel.

*BANG! BANG! BANG!* "ORDER! ORDER!"

Calm was restored to the court.

"There will be no more throwing of rotten fruit in my courtroom," he ordered.

"Someone just threw some tomatoes. They're vegetables aren't they?" asked Thumbs.

"No, tomatoes are fruit!" huffed Fingers, wiping tomato juice off his face.

"I am pretty sure they are vegetables."

"NO! TOMATOES ARE FRUIT, YOU IGNORAMUS!"

"Are they?" Thumbs asked the court.

"YES!" shouted everyone.

"Oh, you learn something new every day," mused Thumbs.

"Now, will the accused please—" said the judge.

Just then an egg **w h i z z e d** through the air and burst on Mr Big's nose.

*CRAC**K**!*

"Ow!" screamed the crime boss.

"Who threw that?" demanded the judge.

No one spoke up.

"I said, 'Who threw that?'"

Again no one said a thing.

"This trial will not begin until the person who threw that egg owns up."

Eventually Reverend Judith put her hand up.

**"YOU, VICAR?!"** exclaimed the judge.

"Sorry, Your Honour," replied the vicar. "But you said no more throwing rotten fruit. I assumed a rotten egg was fine."

Gales of laughter filled the courtroom.

**"HA! HA! HA! HA! HA! HA! HA! HA! HA! HA! HA! HA! HA! HA! HA! HA!"**

"Excuse me, please. I brought along a rotten cabbage," piped up Raj. "That is a vegetable. Is it all right if I throw that, Mr Judge, sir?"

# "NO!" bellowed the judge.

## "No throwing of any foodstuff!"

"Understood. If anyone wants to buy the rotten cabbage from me I will take anything upwards of one p."

# "SILENCE!"

"SHUSH!" shushed Raj to all those around him, though he was the only one who'd been talking.

"Will the accused please stand?" ordered the judge.

The three stood.

"Mr Big, I said 'please stand'!"

The little man scowled.

"I am standing, Your Holiness."

"I am terribly sorry," replied the judge. "Now, you three are charged with robbing a bank. How do you plead? Guilty or not guilty?"

Thumbs popped his hand up. "What do you say when you've done it, but you don't want anyone to know you've done it?"

"Not guilty," replied the judge.

"Not guilty, then," said Thumbs.

Mr Big and Fingers looked at him. He had dropped them all right in it.

# CHAPTER 64

# THE TRUTH

Needless to say, it didn't take long for the jury to reach their verdict.

"GUILTY!" called the jury's foreman.

"I sentence you all to life in prison!" announced the judge, banging his gavel.

The crowd gathered in the courtroom erupted into cheers.

"HOORAY!"

A rotten cabbage flew through the air...

*WHIZZ!*

...and hit Mr Big on the chin.

*CRUNCH!*

"OOF!" shouted the man.

"Sorry! My hand slipped!" called out Raj.

"Take them down!" ordered the judge.

The three glared at Frank as they were led away. "Your daddy is going to get it," shouted Mr Big.

"Who are you talking about?" demanded Judge Pillar.

"If I may, Your Honour?" asked Frank, politely putting his hand up to speak. "Mr Big is talking about my father, Mr Gilbert Goodie. You sentenced him to ten years in prison for the first robbery at the bank. A robbery these men made him commit."

"Did they?"

"Yes, Your Honour. They threatened to hurt me – his son  – if he refused to drive the getaway car."

There were boos from the courtroom and cries of, "SHAME ON THEM!"

The judge **banged** his gavel on the desk. "SILENCE! Where is your father?"

"In prison, Your Honour," replied Frank.

"Oh yes, of course. Silly me," said the judge. Then he called out to one of his clerks, "Bring Gilbert Goodie to this court at once!"

✻

Within the hour, Dad had been taken out of **Wrongfoot Prison**, and rushed to the court in the back of a prison van. Now he was sitting in the dock where the three gang members had been earlier.

"Mr Goodie, it has been proved that you drove the getaway car in the first robbery," began the judge.

"That is correct, Your Honour," replied Dad.

"But your son tells us that Mr Big and his gang threatened to hurt him unless you played your part."

"He spoke the truth, sir. And my boy is the most *precious* thing in the world to me. He is all I've got."

Dad smiled over to his son in the gallery.

"And it's clear you played no part at all in the second robbery."

"No part at all. How could I, Your Honour? I was locked up in prison."

"On this point, I would like to call a guard at **Wrongfoot Prison** to give evidence."

"FETCH MR SWIVEL!" shouted one of the clerks.

The doors swung open, and Mr Swivel took to the stand.

"Yes, I can confirm that Mr Goodie was in prison the whole time, Your Honour," said the prison guard. "Nothing and nobody gets past me."

"Thank you, Mr Swivel," replied the judge. "Well, Mr Goodie, the money from the first bank robbery in which you were forced to play a part has been returned. And it is clear there is no way you could have been involved in the second robbery as you were in **Wrongfoot Prison** at the time. So I have some good news for you, Mr Goodie…"

Dad and Frank's eyes met across the courtroom. The plan had worked a treat! But before the judge could finish, Sergeant Scoff waltzed into the courtroom with a long package under his arm.

"Well, well, well…" announced the policeman. "Gilbert Goodie seems to have fooled you all good and proper."

"WHAT IS THE MEANING OF THIS INTERRUPTION, OFFICER?" thundered the judge.

"Let's not let this man 'hop' free just yet," said Scoff with a grin, clearly delighted with his pun. "He did take part in the robbery last night, and I can prove it!"

"HOW?"

"He left something at the crime scene!"

"WHAT?"

"I don't know if he was drunk, but he was clearly 'legless'."

Dad began fidgeting nervously in his chair. Frank could hardly breathe. This was agonising.

"What on earth are you on about, you strange little man?" demanded the judge.

"His fatal mistake is going to cost him an arm and a leg. Well, at least a leg."

"Will you shut up?" ordered the judge.

"No! I will not shut up! Because the man you may be about to pardon left this at the scene of the crime!"

With that, Scoff unwrapped the package, and held Dad's wooden leg aloft.

Everyone in the courtroom was shocked.

## GASP!

**Dad was done for.**

# CHAPTER

**65**

# FRANK TAKES THE STAGE

"If I may say a few words on behalf of my father, Your Honour?" said Frank.

"This is highly irregular, young man," replied the judge.

"I know I am just a kid, but I think I have something very important to say."

Cries of support came from the crowd of onlookers in the court.

*"LET THE BOY SPEAK!"*

"GIVE HIM A CHANCE!"

**"LET'S HEAR WHAT HE HAS TO SAY!"**

"THIS IS BETTER THAN THE TV!"

"CAN YOU ALL HOLD FOR A MOMENT? I NEED A PEE!"

The judge caved in. "Yes, yes, all right, then, child. Come to the dock, and you can say your piece. But please be brief."

"Thank you, Your Honour," said the boy, before racing down the staircase. Once he'd taken up his position next to his father, he began to explain. "When my father was sentenced to ten years in prison for a bank robbery, you, Your Honour, labelled him a '**bad dad**'. Would a **bad dad** want to put food on the table for his son? Would a **bad dad**

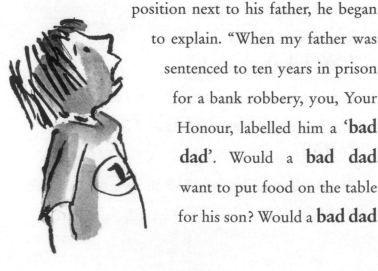

want to scrape some money together to buy his son a present for Christmas? Would a **bad dad** want to make sure his son didn't have to go to school in shoes that were falling apart?"

The courtroom fell silent.

"No. That is not a **bad dad**. My father has brought me up on his own after my mum walked out. He was forced into being the getaway driver for the first bank robbery. Dad had borrowed money because he had no choice. Mr Big and his gang threatened to hurt me if he didn't pay back a hundred times what he had borrowed. He couldn't. My father had to do what this evil gang told him."

Raj was bawling his eyes out...

# "WHAAA!"

...and blowing his nose loudly on a tissue, making a noise like an elephant.

## *TOOT!*

"If myself and the jury had known all this, the outcome of the first trial might have been different," said the judge. "Very different."

"Thank you, Your Honour. But my dad didn't squeal on Mr Big and his gang because they said they would hurt me if he did."

"As a father myself, and a grandfather, I am shocked and **horrified**," replied Judge Pillar.

"Once he was sent to prison, I made a plan for him to escape for just one night. I thought being locked up would be the perfect alibi. Together, we returned all the money that was stolen to the bank. Every last penny."

Mr Swivel's eyes swivelled in his head. This could not be true!

"When we went to put the money back, Mr Big and his henchmen followed us to the bank. So we did something the police of this town could never do. We caught this gang of criminals red-handed."

All eyes turned to Sergeant Scoff, who looked as if he wished the ground would swallow him up.

"That leg that Sergeant Scoff is waving around was

used to shut Mr Big and his henchmen in the vault of the bank. My father sacrificed his own leg, well, his wooden one, so these criminals who have terrorised this town for so long could be brought to justice. He had to hop all the way home."

This caused a ripple of sympathy.

# "Ahhh!"

"Right now he is being held up by nothing more than an old plastic mop."

Dad rolled up his trouser leg to reveal the rather sorry-looking mop.

This caused a tidal wave of sympathy.

# "Ahhhhh!"

Reverend Judith and Auntie Flip were both in bits. The two ladies were now sitting next to each other and sharing a lace handkerchief. They looked a little surprised to find that, without thinking, they'd wrapped their arms round each other.

"So this isn't a **bad dad**. This is a good dad. A really good dad. In fact, he's the best dad in the world. And I'm proud to call him my dad."

Frank looked at his father from across the courtroom. Both had tears in their eyes. As hard as it was for the boy to find the words, it was harder still for his father to listen to them. People so rarely ever say what they really truly feel in their heart.

All eyes turned to Judge Pillar.

"I have listened with great interest to what you have had to say. Nothing can escape the fact that your father did drive the getaway car in a bank robbery. However, there are circumstances of which the court was unaware at the first trial. Circumstances that shine a whole new light on this case. Your father has served two months in prison. That is quite enough. Today the court is giving him a full pardon. From this moment, he is a FREE MAN!"

The court erupted into wild applause and cheers as Sergeant Scoff stamped his foot and stormed out.

Dad opened up his arms and Frank ran towards him.
The man scooped the boy up and spun him round.
Dad held on to his son tightly.

**"I love you, mate,"**

he whispered into Frank's ear.

**"And I love you."**

# CHAPTER

# NOT A SEAT
# IN THE HOUSE

"I love you."

"And I love you."

It was six months later, and Frank and his father were sitting in church listening to two other people say those three words to each other. It was the marriage of Reverend Judith and Auntie Flip. The happy couple looked into each other's eyes and kissed.

"My first kiss!" exclaimed Auntie Flip.

"And certainly not your last," said Judith.

The wedding guests all clapped and cheered. Finally the town's church was full of people.

Raj was in the front row, bawling his eyes out again.

The church roof was leaking again too. Rainwater dripped on the two brides, though it didn't dampen their spirits. Both ladies were smiling like never before.

"I have written a poem!" announced Auntie Flip.

"Oh no," said Frank under his breath.

"It's called '*My Lovely Judith*'.

 "*I was always very prudish*
*Until I met Judith.*
*It's all been a surprise;*
*She has opened my eyes*
*To a world of love.*
*I feel like a dove,*
 *Not a magician's one hidden up a sleeve,*
*No – one that is floating on the breeze,*
*Soaring happy and free*
*For all the world to see.*"

The wedding guests all erupted into wild applause.

"That wasn't bad," said Dad.

"I take it back!" said Frank.

Auntie Flip looked overwhelmed by the reaction of the crowd.

"Thank you, thank you. I have written seventeen more," she said.

"Let's save them for another day," Judith jumped in. The vicar smiled at her new bride. "Now, as you can see, the church roof is still in dire need of repair, so no wedding gifts, please. Instead, we are going to have a collection now for the church roof. So, if you have any loose change, please pop it on the tray when it comes round. Thank you."

"Have you got any money on you, Dad?" asked Frank.

The man rolled up his trousers to reveal his false leg.

"Dad, what are you doing?"

"You'll see."

He slid back a block of wood to reveal a secret compartment in his leg. It was stuffed full of crisp fifty-pound notes.

"Where did you get those from?" asked the boy.

"Mr Big's safe, of course!"

"But you said—"

"I know, mate. I'm sorry. I took a wad out of the safe when you weren't looking. Hid it in my leg. There's enough there to repair the church roof, and of course a tiny bit left over for us!"

**"Bad Dad!"** joked Frank.

**"Good Dad!"** replied Dad.

"Pass it here."

Dad did so, and Frank looked at the stack of fifty-pound notes in his hand. The money wasn't beautiful. It was ugly, or at least it made people do ugly things. As the tray came round to their row, Frank plonked the whole lot down and passed it on.

"**MATE!**" exclaimed Dad. "What are you doing?"

"We don't need it, Dad. It's only brought trouble."

"But—"

"No buts. It's not going to make us happy."

"I guess you are right, mate," agreed Dad as he watched the tray disappear out of sight with longing in his eyes.

*DING DONG DING DONG!*
*DING DONG DING DONG!*

The bells rang out for the end of the wedding service.

When the guests exited the church, Frank was astonished to see that a Mini with a Union Jack emblazoned on it was waiting for them.

"**Queenie**?" asked Frank. "It can't be! She was flattened by the crane."

"It's **Queenie II**!" replied Dad. "I salvaged everything I could, and added some bits from the scrapyard. Her heart is still the same, though."

"Why didn't you tell me?"

"I wanted to keep it a surprise for the newlyweds."

"Oh, thank you so much, Gilbert!" exclaimed Reverend Judith.

"What a super way to drive to the seaside honeymoon! Thank you, thank you, thank you!" added Auntie Flip. "It almost makes up for me having to spend a night in prison for you!"

"Sorry about that," said Frank.

"So who wants to drive?" asked Dad, dangling the car keys.

"I'll drive!" said Auntie Flip.

"No, no, I'll drive!" said Reverend Judith.

"They are having their first argument as a married couple!" observed Raj as he threw what looked like confetti over them. "That didn't take long."

Auntie Flip started trying to pick the pieces out of her hair. "What is this stuff, Raj?"

"Oh, I had some mini marshmallows that were well past their sell-by date, so I thought I would use them instead."

"Thank you, Raj," replied Reverend Judith with a hint of sarcasm as she picked the gloopy balls out of her hair. "We can eat these later."

"I wouldn't," said the newsagent. "They were going **mouldy**."

"Eurgh!"

The crowd waved as the car zoomed off down the street.

## ROAR!

"Careful! I need her back in one piece!" shouted Dad after them.

"You aren't going to race her again?" asked Frank.

"No, you are, mate."

"*Me?*"

"Yeah! If you want to. You are a ruddy good driver already."

"Thanks, Dad."

"And I can teach you everything I know."

The boy smiled. **"We make a good team, Dad."**

**"We certainly do, mate."**

The pair walked away from the church.

"Your mother sent me a letter," began Dad.

"Oh yes?" replied the boy.

"She wants to pop over to the flat next week. Just for a cup of tea. See how you are. What do you think?"

Frank pondered this. "Yes. A cup of tea. I think that's a good start."

"A fresh start," replied Dad.

"We'll have to ask her to bring a tea bag, though," joked Frank.

"And some milk."

"And sugar!"

"And hot water."

"Apart from that we've got everything we need to make the perfect cup of tea!"

# CHAPTER

# 67

# WISH

As Frank and his father crossed the park on their way back to their block of flats, they passed the wishing well. Dad searched deep in his trouser pockets for a coin. He found a penny.

"This is all I've got, mate," said Dad. "Do you want to make a wish? Like old times?"

He held out his hand for his son to take the coin. Frank looked at it.

"I don't need to make a wish."

"Why?"

"I've got nothing left to wish for. All I ever wanted, all I ever needed, was you. My dad."

**"You are my best mate, son."**

**"And you are my best mate, Dad.** Always and forever. Now come on."

"Where are we going?"

"Raj's!" exclaimed the boy. "We have a whole one p to splash out with!"

"You better not spend it all at once!"

The pair of best friends shared a smile, and walked off together with their arms round each other in a very special **huggle**.

*They may have only had **one pence** to spend, but their hearts beamed with gold.*